ABOUT NECROMANCY

Can a book animate the dead?

When dead bugs start flying and a ghost becomes corporeal, all signs point to yes.

The effects of the book are contained...for now. Europe's other world policing agency, frantic for a way to stop the effects of the book's magic before it spreads, turn to the library's most promising spell caster, Lizzie, for help.

But can Lizzie wrestle the evil book into submission before it sparks an undead uprising?

NECROMANCY

A LOST LIBRARY STORY

KATE BARAY

1

What was that saying about cake and eating it? It had never made sense to Lizzie. Of course if you had cake, you'd want to eat it. It was *cake*.

But right now, she got it. Today, in this moment, it was crystal freaking clear.

She'd made a trade.

Her special talents were to be applied to a particular problem, and in exchange, her boss Harrington would apply *his* special talents to her best friend Kenna's problem.

At the time, it had seemed reasonable. Okay...not reasonable, but it had been her and Kenna's only option. Kenna's mom Gwen—a truly badass lady—had been kidnapped. Harrington had agreed to exert what influence he wielded as one of the top brass in the Inter-Pack Policing Cooperative to resolve the situation.

And all she had to do was solve a little problem for IPPC.

Since IPPC was her sometimes employer and she loved Gwen like a mother, there hadn't been any debate at all. She'd said yes.

She'd done it willingly and without complaint.

"You sorry, bastard! Die. Die, you sonofabitch!" Her throat burned from screaming.

Maybe she should take it down a notch.

Nah. She was having a few regrets about that hastily struck deal, and screaming her lungs out was a great tension reliever. Which reminded her of the other kind of tension relieving she wouldn't be getting anytime soon, because her fiancé was stuck in Texas.

While she screamed bloody murder in a small, dark room in the basement of an old house in Prague, John was kicking wolf butt in Texas and making sure the Pack minded their Ps and Qs.

She could be oversimplifying the job of Alpha, but she was also cranky. She hated wasps, and the nasty dead-and-alive-again creatures were currently dive-bombing her. "I am going to smear your innards across the wall, you flying menace!"

And this was where the *cake* and the *eating of cake* came in. She was realizing she wanted her cake (Harrington's help) and the eating of it (a really easy, quickly resolved IPPC job, preferably with John nearby to help). An impossibility.

Harrington would never have negotiated her help in exchange for an easy job. Harrington didn't *do* small jobs. And on the off chance she was wrong and he lowered himself to resolve the more menial of IPPC's crises, he certainly wasn't calling her in to help.

Maybe, one day, in a far-distant and rose-colored future, Harrington would call her in for a different kind of case. The kind without dead things coming alive again, with no evil geniuses in sight, and no masterminds plotting to take over the magical world.

"Take that!" she snarled as she hopped on one foot and smacked the wall and an undead wasp with her shoe. This would be a lot easier if they had more than the dim emergency lights.

"Lizzie, yelling doesn't help." Pilar's exasperated voice echoed in the barren chamber.

"It makes me feel better." And eased her frustration ever so slightly. Even though Lizzie knew that an easy job for IPPC didn't exist, that didn't make her frustration disappear. As for the cake-eating imagery...she was hungry. She wasn't a pleasant hungry person in the best of circumstances. "Die, you flying little shits. Die!"

Yelling definitely helped. Hopping on one foot, not so much. She stopped to put her shoe back on and then crushed one of the earthbound bugs.

"Honey, I think we can safely assume these things aren't dying anytime soon." Pilar directed her flashlight toward the latest victim of Lizzie's rampage.

It had been a beetle, until she'd smashed it. Was *still* a beetle. A squashed zombie version of its former self, but a beetle nonetheless.

"We've squished them, flattened them, and beaten them." Lizzie winced at the whiny turn her voice had taken. She cleared her throat, which made it ache all the more, and said, "They should be dead a few times over."

"Will you finally fess up and agree that the zombie apocalypse is upon us?" Pilar asked.

The way she said "zombie apocalypse" in her precise and only slightly accented voice reminded Lizzie more of cute get-togethers with matching linens and scones than the end of the world as they knew it.

She flicked a desiccated, unidentifiable bug away with her toe and swatted away yet another fly. The thing only had one wing. How could a one-winged insect fly? "You were talking about a bug-zombie apocalypse. It just didn't seem like a thing."

"It's a thing." Pilar swung her flashlight around the enclosed chamber, illuminating a number of flying insects and several of the crawling variety, all in various stages of decomposition—or regeneration, depending on one's point of view.

"Yeah, you've convinced me. Bugpocalypse is a thing." Lizzie flicked her flashlight beam along the lines marked on the wooden floors. They moved out in concentric circles from a point in the middle of the room. Each line represented the passage of six hours.

Why six? She didn't know. What she did know was that bugpocalypse was spreading. At an even and not particularly fast pace, but certainly spreading. That was the purpose of the circles, to track the spread of necromantic magic. Someone—not Pilar, perhaps Harrington himself?—had come up with the fabulous idea of seeding the room with the corpses of dead insects. She'd initially hoped they weren't being murdered for that purpose, since there were plenty of the naturally occurring variety lying about.

Even though they were bugs, it still seemed cruel. Or so Lizzie had thought *before* they'd started to crawl on her, fly into her hair, and generally make aggressive nuisances of themselves. Killing the little buggers sounded just fine to her now.

Her scalp crawled, and she patted her hair—just in case. She'd tossed it in a ponytail, per Pilar's advice. Seemed to be clear, but she'd likely have nightmares about undead bugs getting tangled in her hair for days.

With a shiver, she returned her attention to the lines on the floor. The furthest mark was still several feet from the walls or door. Thankfully, bugpocalypse hadn't breached the walls of this small, hidden room. This particular chamber had been constructed specifically for the purpose of housing and studying the more dangerous books. It was located in the basement of the IPPC building, next to the supposed secret library that was becoming less secret all the time.

With any luck, the powers that be at IPPC (primarily Harrington) could continue to keep this top-secret research room under wraps. Keeping bugpocalypse confined within its walls—or, rather, stopping the undead uprising of insects—was Lizzie and Pilar's job.

Her beam traveled over the smallest circle and then further to the podium in the center of it. An old book rested on the flat surface. Black, leather-bound, plain. Nothing special, other than its age and, oh yeah, its ability to bring dead stuff back to life.

"Tell me who thought it was a good idea to poke

around inside a book on necromancy?" Lizzie asked. She knew the answer, because who else could it be?

Unlike Kenna, Lizzie tried to give Harrington the benefit of the doubt. He was a good man. Deep down, under a thick layer of ambition that he harnessed to pursue IPPC's goals. Deep, deep down.

He'd yanked her away from the love of her life just as they were establishing a fine balance between the commitments in each of their lives. And he had also pulled her away from her best friend in a time of extreme crisis.

Extreme crisis, doubled: Gwen's forthcoming trial and Kenna's very unexpected pregnancy.

Yeah, really, *really* deep down, he was a decent guy.

Pilar shot her a knowing look. "Harrington approved it, but it wasn't Harrington pushing for the work on that book. I know it's hard to believe. He approached the project with caution and only approved it after assurances from the transcriber convinced him the risk was minimal."

"Oh." Lizzie pushed away the prick of guilt she felt. She shouldn't feel bad. The blame for all things IPPC and overreaching could usually be laid at Harrington's door. He was the man behind the curtain, when it came to any activity geared toward increasing IPPC's power and knowledge base.

"She was convinced there was no danger," Pilar said, "and there weren't any problems initially. She worked on it for several days without incident."

"What changed?"

Pilar sighed. "Nothing that we know of. One moment

she was unlocking some text, and the next we had bugs coming back to life. And before you ask, the text was some simple biographical data, not a trap, so far as we can tell."

Lizzie nodded. She'd worked with spelled books enough at this point to know that the record keeper working on the transcription would have felt the magical rush if she'd sprung a trap. "I'd like to talk to her. Can you set up an interview?"

"Not possible. That particular record keeper is taking a lengthy vacation, from which she will return to another posting."

"Harrington's doing?" Working in the library was a plum job, and only the most qualified and trustworthy record keepers were included in the rotation of staff. To have access to all the awesomeness of the library and then...not—that was a harsh punishment indeed.

That was the second time she'd leaped to a negative conclusion about Harrington. Kenna's dislike of the man was wearing off on Lizzie. And it didn't help that she missed John.

"More a requirement for her continued mental well-being. She wasn't handling the situation very well." Pilar clicked her flashlight off. "You ready to get out of here? This place makes my skin crawl, and I'm amazed I've managed to avoid a bug up my nose this long."

"That, or we could get stung by a zombie wasp." Lizzie held her flashlight under her chin. "Would that turn us into zombies?"

"Bite your tongue."

Lizzie grinned at her friend and mentor. Bad as

zombie bugs were, they'd at least partially distracted her from the more personal catastrophe that was currently unfolding. The grin slipped away as the full weight of Gwen's kidnapping settled on her again. "Let's get out of here. I've seen enough to be convinced, and I need to check on Kenna."

"You don't want to examine the book?" Pilar asked.

"And risk triggering an even worse event than bugpocalypse? I'll think I'll hold off for now." Lizzie's stomach grumbled. "Pilar, how do you feel about cake?"

2

———

Turned out Pilar wasn't so keen on cake for breakfast. She passed quite forcefully when Lizzie mentioned it.

Elin, IPPC's eager intern from Norway, caught Lizzie and Pilar debating the merits of cake for breakfast and didn't even try to contain her amusement.

"Cake or eggs for breakfast?" Lizzie asked the girl as they passed.

"Cake, of course. It's too good to refuse at any hour." Elin grinned, revealing a dimple.

The rosy cheeks, the dimple, and the yellow-blonde hair combined with her enthusiasm made her seem even younger than her sixteen years. If Lizzie hadn't met her while she was helping Kenna with research and seen her proficiency as a spell caster, she'd have questioned the presence of such a young girl on the premises.

"Your internship is going well?" Pilar asked. Sneaky woman. She wanted to escape a crushing defeat in the cake-breakfast debate and was diverting the conversation accordingly.

"Yes, very well. Thank you." Elin blushed, and her gaze skittered away. She clasped her hands together, squeezed them tight, and then blurted, "Am I going to get a chance to see the book?"

She looked like a little girl asking for confirmation that Santa was real and fearing the answer might be unpleasant. Lizzie didn't want to crush the girl's dreams; better to let Pilar do that. She turned and waited for Pilar to respond.

"You know you don't have clearance. I'm sorry, Elin. You should be grateful that you get to work with the less dangerous books. It's an amazing opportunity."

The girl's smile didn't hide her disappointment. "Yes. I'm thankful for the opportunity." She bit her lip, clearly wanting to say more. She hesitated then shook her head, and the moment was lost. "Lizzie, Mr. Harrington just finished debriefing Kenna, and I think he wanted to speak with you."

Elin and Pilar headed down to the main library to do what research they could on the bug problem. Not that they hadn't already searched, but the library was vast and, as yet, not fully catalogued, so there was still hope that a nugget might be buried amid the old tomes.

As Elin and Pilar headed off to dig through the archives, Lizzie headed to Harrington's office and contemplated cake.

Not everyone could handle all that sugar so early in the day. That and her ability to practically consume her own weight in bacon were two of Lizzie's favorite non-magical talents.

First cake, now bacon; she had food on the brain.

And apparently couldn't keep it to herself, based on Harrington's greeting when she arrived. "Why are you mumbling about bacon?" Harrington peered at her from behind his monstrosity of a desk. "Do I need to have a tray sent in?"

While Pilar had been giving Lizzie a firsthand look at her latest assignment, Harrington had finished briefing Kenna on the help IPPC would be giving her as she attempted to retrieve her kidnapped mother. Even thinking about it made Lizzie break out in a sweat. Thoughts of cake and bacon and disappointed Norwegian interns fled.

She would not let the pressure get to her. She *never* let the pressure get to her.

The beauty of being inundated by one crisis after another, she supposed. Since she'd joined the magical community, her life had been a whirlwind. In good and bad ways, but she'd not been alone through any of it, and she wasn't now.

Harrington's help was the reason she was here in his office now.

Typical of his usual management style, he'd moved on to the next crisis: bugpocalypse. The man switched from one emergency to another like he was flipping channels on a TV.

He shook his head then retrieved an energy bar from his desk drawer. He tended to assume an air of exasperation whenever she or Kenna was near. A subtle air, because Harrington was still Harrington, closed-off emotions and all.

"Catch," he said a split second before chucking the bar at her.

She did, one-handed. Then ripped into the snack like it was the cake she'd been fantasizing about all morning. As she swallowed the last bite, she considered whether she should add improving her diet to her mental to-do list. When she considered the sweet, buttery goodness of cake and the crisp, savory awesomeness of perfectly fried bacon, that decision seemed unlikely.

She blinked. That was a lot of food love, even for her. Maybe she was more than a wee bit stressed. And tired. Unlike Kenna, she hadn't slept on the plane for more than a few minutes at a time. "Uh, thanks. I might have been a little hungry. So, what were you were saying about paying Gwen's ransom?"

He so hadn't said that. He'd said exactly the *opposite* of that.

He steepled his fingers. "Not happening." She took a breath, readying herself to make a pitch, but he nipped her ambitions in the bud. "We don't have access to most of the assets, and regaining control of them would require more stealth and time than I possess. Those assets now reside in the hands of mundane law enforcement."

A pinch in her chest made her breath catch. It wasn't anything she hadn't already known or expected, but it still sucked. When she could speak, she said, "You can't let anything happen to Gwen."

"I'm helping. I said I would, and I am."

The implication was clear: he stuck by his word, and it was time for her to do the same.

"Tell me everything you know about bugpocalypse, just in case Pilar missed something." She sent a silent apology out to Pilar. If anything had been missed, it had been because a sleepy, hungry Lizzie had zoned out a few times. But only up until they'd entered the freaky room of dead things. Then she'd been completely awake. "And send for coffee. I definitely need coffee."

Harrington raised an eyebrow but didn't comment on her switch from tea to coffee. At least she hadn't requested hot chocolate. That usually meant she was two seconds from a meltdown. She didn't envision Harrington dealing well with tears, sobbing, and hysterics.

After making a quick call down to the kitchen, Harrington proceeded to give her the background for bugpocalypse. He skipped the part where the book containing necromantic magic was originally discovered, since she'd been the one to discover the secret library's even more secret stash of dangerous books. Death magic, blood magic—Vampyrs were the worst—and necromancy, three sorts of magic that most magic-users wouldn't touch with a ten-foot pole.

After a brief overview of the initial work the "vacationing" record keeper had done, Harrington said, "It shouldn't be possible. The book alone can't be bringing these creatures back to life. No matter how small they are, it takes an enormous amount of magic to reanimate the dead. Sparking life, even life as limited as, say, a zombie bug, is a herculean effort."

"Okay." She mentally reviewed the staff she knew, and no one stood out as suspicious. "You've had Ewan double- or triple-check staff backgrounds? No evil geniuses lurking? No one with a psychotic grudge against insects? Actually, I guess that would be a peculiar fondness for them, since they're being reanimated."

Harrington's lips twitched—whether in amusement or annoyance, she couldn't tell—and he replied, "That *would* fall under the chief of security's job description."

When he failed to elaborate, she asked, "How about a list of people who've had access to the book?" Even as she asked, she knew the list would be prohibitively short: Harrington, herself, Pilar, the missing record keeper, and perhaps Ewan. "Or even anyone who's been in the vicinity since the zombie bugs appeared. That would include access to the main library, since they share a wall."

"All above reproach, since IPPC library employees are screened even more closely than other IPPC branches." He quirked an eyebrow. "Perhaps you or Pilar have taken a sudden interest in reanimation? But the list is short: you, Pilar, myself, Ewan, two of his security team, a trusted spell caster—"

"Who's currently on vacation."

He nodded. "Elin, our intern. Our librarian, Emme, who would normally have access, happens to be away at the moment. Everyone on the list has been quite thoroughly vetted, but I encourage you to discuss any concerns with Ewan."

"Where's Emme?"

Harrington frowned.

"It's just that Elin is her niece, so I'd have thought she would want to keep an eye on her, keep her out of trouble, that sort of thing, while the girl is interning. You have to admit that IPPC isn't the safest of places to work."

She didn't mention bugpocalypse, because that was just the latest in a series of dangerous events happening in and around IPPC.

"Emme is taking a vacation. She's been working overtime for weeks now, developing a system equipped to handle our books."

Lizzie still thought it was weird, but she let it go for now. She'd ask Elin about her aunt later.

Besides, Ewan was damn good at his job and would have checked out anything unusual. Job competency was just one perk when you lived longer than the rest of the inhabitants of the planet.

Lizzie hadn't a clue what the average life span of a dragon was, but she knew Ewan had been around a *long* time. Additionally, she knew most of the people on the list, all but the vacationing spell caster.

She huffed out a frustrated breath. "Someone is powering the book. Can't you just—"

A knock on the door was quickly followed by the arrival of her coffee. What turned out to be her perfectly prepared coffee. She needed to eat some real food, but this would do for now. She didn't exactly love the stuff, but desperate times and all that. Tea just wasn't going to cut it for her current level of exhaustion.

"Elizabeth." Harrington's dry tone cut into the brief moment of pleasure. "You were saying?"

She hated when people used her full name as if she were a misbehaving child.

What had she been saying? Lots of magic required to spark life in dead critters...reviewing staff access to the necromancy book and the library in general... "Oh, right. So, with all of the sophisticated spell casters you have running around, don't you have someone who can cast a sensing ward and then trace the magic that's feeding into the book back to the source? Culprit found, disaster averted, and I can get back to helping Kenna rescue her mom."

So simple. Beautifully simple.

Harrington leaned forward and rested his arms on his desk. "Reason has not completely deserted me. Not only has Pilar attempted a sensing ward, but I've even done so myself. None of our efforts have been rewarded. To be clear: we found *nothing*."

Of course he'd tried to locate the source with a sensing ward. He'd have been an idiot not to. But they found nothing? And Harrington was good. Wicked good. "I don't understand how that's possible. Nothing, as in no magic trail?"

"Nothing, as in no *magic*. Well, nothing beyond the very small amount to be found in any magical book."

She shook her head slowly. "I don't understand. You just told me that reanimation requires massive amounts of magic. You just said to reanimate *one* of those creepy little zombie bug dudes would require a lot of magic, and we've got bugpocalypse rolling under our feet. There must be a hundred or more bugs that have been reani-mated, and you can't find any magic?"

"That is indeed what I am attempting to convey."

"That's not possible."

"No, it is not. Or, rather, it's not within our understanding of the possible."

She slurped the last of the coffee in her cup, then started pacing. "What does my aunt Matylda think?"

Matylda wasn't actually her aunt, more like her great-great- (she forgot how many greats) aunt, but that had quickly become too complicated.

Harrington pushed his chair away from his desk and crossed his arms. "I was hoping you would tell me."

She halted mid-stride and did an about-face. "You haven't heard from her?" When he just stared, she said, "I haven't heard from her either."

Her toe started to tap, a good sign the coffee was doing its job. She looked down at her foot, then the floor, and then tried to calculate exactly what was below her feet. For example, was the super-secret chamber that had housed Matylda's spirit for centuries down there? Where was it? How close was her former resting place to—

"Oh, hell. Tell me Matylda's room is nowhere near the room of dead bugs and the big, bad book. Please."

She'd never had good spatial awareness, but right now she was doing her damnedest to recall what she knew of the chamber's location. Months ago, she'd discovered several taboo books inside it, along with Matylda's remains.

Small problem: she'd *faded* to the location. Fade, teleport, or translocate. Pick one, but they all meant the same thing. Lizzie hadn't a clue where the chamber was located, because she'd magically zapped her way inside it with a great deal of guidance from Matylda. She only knew it was somewhere underground and completely inaccessible without the ability to fade inside its walls.

Matylda had been buried alive in that room. She'd died in that room. And her corpse had lain, untouched, in that same room until Lizzie had found her.

Given the state of the bug corpses sharing a room with the necromancy book, Lizzie hoped Matylda's secret chamber was far, far away from that cursed book.

"Please tell me this crazy reanimation plague could not be affecting Matylda in some way." Lizzie firmly tamped down the anxiety burbling in her chest.

Matylda was a hundreds-year-old ghost. What harm could come to her? And her resting place might be nowhere near the necromancy book and the spreading bugpocalypse.

But Lizzie's anxiety refused to be squashed like the pest it was. Oh, God. Terrible analogy. Terrible.

"We haven't heard boo from her since the first reanimation sighting."

Was that Harrington trying to be funny? If it was, she might have to consider slowly suffocating him. She had a handy ward that would do exactly that. She eyed him critically, trying to decide if he was feeling punny or if it had been a slip of the tongue. "Ohmigod, I'm channeling Kenna."

Harrington scowled. "Don't start throwing things at me."

It was a little terrifying that he got that reference so quickly. Lizzie exhaled, trying in vain to release some tension. A missing ghost aunt was a bad, bad thing in the midst of bugpocalypse. She rubbed her engagement ring, a ring that had once belonged to Matylda.

She twisted it around finger a few times and concentrated on Matylda, but nothing happened. She liked to think the pretty sapphire ring had forged a connection of sorts between the two of them. That it helped her to reach out to Matylda, or vice versa.

Fat lot of good it was doing her now.

Her pacing feet brought her back to the chair she'd previously occupied, and she collapsed into it. "I haven't heard from her, you haven't heard from her, and we have dead stuff crawling around all over the place. We're not exactly sure where that super-secret room is, are we, Harrington?"

He didn't argue.

She'd hoped IPPC had a general idea. The only way into or out of the doorless room was to fade, and it wasn't like they had architectural plans for the super-secret room where the illegal books were stashed. That was the whole point: no one was supposed to know the place existed.

"This is not good, Harrington. Matylda is special. She's family." Lizzie gave him the stink eye. "She better not be hurt, or—" She couldn't help but think of the maimed bugs crawling and the one-winged fly still flitting around. "She better not be...different. You know, less ghostly."

That was as close to articulating what she was thinking as she could manage. The words *zombie aunt* and *walking corpse* were not passing her lips.

She huffed out an agitated breath.

Dangit. Kenna really was rubbing off on Lizzie. She was all sorts of pissed, and perfectly content to direct all of her angst at Harrington.

The guy in charge of the library.

The guy who okayed the questionable probe of the necromancy book.

He deserved some blame, and he'd be getting more than that if anything happened to Matylda.

Harrington returned her heated look with calm detachment. "She's a ghost, Lizzie. It would be difficult to harm her."

"Says you."

"You've seen the markings on the floor. Each mark records the furthest point of reanimation after a six-hour period. The effects of the magic are spreading, but in a slow and relatively predictable manner. Unless the chamber of your aunt's death is located very near to the room we constructed to study the book, then she won't even be exposed."

Serious stink eye, that was what Lizzie was sending Harrington's way.

"And that's assuming there's even enough of her to be reanimated." He rose to refill her cup.

She eyed it. Even though her heart was already racing, she took a sip. She had research to do, some serious research that might involve, for all she knew, sparks and stuff exploding. It would definitely involve more creepy-crawly dead things. Caffeine seemed like a good idea.

Whiskey might be better.

She chugged the cooling coffee. "I'm gonna have a closer look at that damn book."

And she was casting her own sensing ward, because even Harrington made mistakes.

Right?

3
———

"Ow is there no magic?" Lizzie had cast three sensing wards in quick succession, not one of which showed any more than the hint of magic to be expected in a magically recorded book.

Nothing at all around, near, or, most especially, trailing away from the necromancy book.

Either her magic was on the fritz or something strange—aliens-invading strange—was going on here.

She eyed the creepy little black book, barely visible in the emergency lighting.

Superficially, it looked innocuous. Except it should be exhibiting signs of magic flowing to, from, or around it. The absence of any significant levels of magic made the thing beyond creepy.

Three times she'd tried, and three times she'd gotten nothing but the mellow glow of a spelled book. A really mellow glow. Even the Texas Pack's book, the one she had stashed safely at home, had more magic juice than this thing, and it was pretty normal as far as magic books went.

To spell a book, a spell caster, a very special kind of spell caster—a record keeper—had to use their magic to tie words to the book. Technically, a record keeper could attach those words to any object, but it required less magic when a book was used to anchor the words. Something to do with the purpose of the spelled object matching up with the purpose of the magic.

Long story short: even if that slim black volume hadn't started bugpocalypse, it was still an old spelled book with some vile tricks up its, uh, spine. Encoding whatever nastiness it held should have required more magic than Lizzie was seeing.

"There should be *more*. Maybe if I touch it?" Or not. Handling the book wouldn't be smart.

Pilar placed her hands on her hips. She was wearing a shift dress and a delicate fitted cardigan, of all things. Without a care for wrinkles or zombie bug guts. "No. No touching."

Lizzie flicked her flashlight up and down Pilar's dress. She and her dress were immaculate.

Lizzie shrugged. She glanced down at her own long-sleeved tee and then quickly looked away. No need to examine the dark splotches too closely, because ewww.

She snorted. She was in the midst of bugpocalypse, and she was cringing over some insect innards on her clothes.

Hands still on her hips, Pilar said, "I'm turning the regular lights on. I really don't see how they could impact the book, and the flickering emergency lights add in the worst possible way to the ambience."

Lizzie didn't argue, because she'd about had enough of feeling like she'd stepped into a horror flick. A few seconds later, Pilar had the lights on.

Lizzie flicked off her flashlight and tucked it in her rear pocket. "I'm going to try another sensing ward. Just to make sure the lights don't make a difference."

Which just seemed weird. Why would electricity running into the room have any effect? But someone had thought so, because emergency protocols required the use of special lighting that wasn't tied into the house's electrical system.

She centered herself, found her magic, and cast another ward. Was that a flash? She blinked, and it was gone. "Did you see that?"

A frown flitted across Pilar's face. "The lights shimmered...perhaps?"

"So you saw it too?" Lizzie examined the overhead lighting. Since they'd turned on the regular lights, there hadn't been any flickering or buzzing, apart from the undead flying insects that still occupied the room.

"Yes. But whether it was the lights, or..." Pilar looked at the black book on the pedestal.

Before either of them could come up with a reasonable explanation or dismiss it as unimportant, Lizzie's phone rang. A glance at the caller ID revealed it was Harrington.

Lizzie contemplated ignoring the call for a split second, but common sense prevailed. "What's going on, bossman?"

A woman replied, "You have to stop. Whatever you're doing, stop now."

Clearly not Harrington. But also not anyone Lizzie knew. "Who—"

"My office. Now," Harrington snapped, and hung up.

Pilar looked around the room. "Perhaps we should turn off the lights on the way out?"

"Sure, but you and I both know that's not the problem." Lizzie bit her lip. "Maybe I shouldn't have gone so crazy with the sensing wards."

She hadn't physically touched the book, but she had cast four wards in total. That was a decent bit of magic.

In a room with a dangerous book.

"Four sensing wards." She winced. "Crap."

Pilar patted her arm. "Hey. We don't know what's happened yet. And besides, I was standing right here. Did you hear me saying it was a bad idea?"

Good point, and Pilar was the queen of common sense.

Lizzie tiptoed away, trying to avoid as many of the crawling nasties on the floor as possible.

Only when she approached the exit did she realize there were no bug corpses. The door was a good seven feet from the last circle marking the effects of the book's necromantic magic, and yet there were no insect corpses littering the floor.

All the bugs in the room were active.

She and Pilar shared a look before hurrying up the last few steps and shoving the door shut behind them.

As they leaned against the door, they looked at one another.

"You saw that," Pilar said.

"Oh, yeah." Hard to miss all the undead things. So many undead things. So many... A shiver traveled up Lizzie's spine. "We have to get to Harrington's office ASAP."

4
———

Lizzie and Pilar made it to Harrington's office in record time. Pilar made pretty good time for a woman wearing heels. Kitten heels, but even so.

Dread settled in Lizzie's stomach as she stood in front of his door, but there was also a hint of excitement intermingled.

She reviewed the brief phone conversation that had precipitated their mad dash—most especially the strange woman's clear and coherent speech—and allowed herself to feel a tiny bit of hope.

She twisted the ring on her finger. Her engagement ring. Matylda's ring.

Panting just a little, Pilar said, "Maybe you should open the door? Since we did bother to rush."

Right. Good plan. Lizzie flung the door open.

Harrington sat behind his desk. A woman sat across from him. Not young, but her exact age was hard to pinpoint. Her clothing dated from some earlier century and was in good condition...all things considered.

A poke in Lizzie's back pushed her into the room, where she was followed by Pilar.

If Lizzie wasn't mistaken, those clothes were exactly as old as they appeared to be, and the woman in the chair calmly studying her was the corporeal form of Matylda Kovar, her many-times-over great-aunt. The same woman who had died in that tiny, sealed chamber where the forbidden books had been stored.

The woman rose gracefully from her chair, followed by Harrington. In a foreign accent with strong British overtones, she said, "Close your mouth, child, you're gawking."

Lizzie snapped her mouth shut. She pressed her lips tightly together, considered whether any other answer was possible, and finally asked, "You're Matylda?"

"I am." Matylda's gaze slid away. "Of a sort."

Lizzie's gaze flicked between Harrington and Matylda. She'd been worried that if Matylda was touched by the necromancy book's magic, she would be altered in some terrible way. She looked pretty good for a dead woman. Other than a paleness bordering on unnatural and a thinness accentuated by her loose clothing, she looked almost...alive. Properly alive, not dead and alive *again*.

Except what had she meant when Lizzie asked if she was Matylda? What kind of answer was "of a sort"?

Lizzie was doing a poor job of hiding her distress—or her sneaky boss was mind reading—because he urged her to sit down with what might even be an expression of concern on his face. Lizzie had secretly (not so secretly) harbored the suspicion that Harrington could mind-read, so she knew which way she was voting.

"I'm good standing. Now what aren't you telling me?" She felt Pilar touch her back in support.

"Your aunt's initial appearance was problematic." This came from a third party, someone in the periphery of the room.

In a chair near Harrington's fireplace, Ewan, the library's chief of security, lounged like a man without a care in the world. Lizzie knew better. He wasn't relaxed, and he certainly wasn't a man. She'd caught a glint of green when his creepy dragon eyes flashed, and she knew he was ready to spring into action.

"Problematic how? And why are you here?" There was a hint of accusation in her tone, but heck, the guy was security, so who could blame her? This was her aunt.

But only "of a sort," according to the woman herself.

She shifted her focus back to Matylda. Lizzie wasn't a huggy person, but she wanted to hug her aunt, even if she wasn't a hundred percent alive. Matylda was the only family connection she had with any magic, and Matylda had always been good people.

"He's here to protect you," Matylda said in a much-too-calm voice.

"All of you," Ewan added.

"Oookay," Lizzie said. She moved to close the gap between herself and Matylda, but Pilar stopped her with a very firm grip on her arm.

Matylda wasn't a danger. Not now, whatever she'd done earlier. But common sense prevailed, and Lizzie waited for the story.

Her posture perfect and her speech precise, Matylda said, "When I initially appeared, before I was fully formed and before my ghostly being had yet to attach itself to my physical form, I attacked a member of the household." She clasped her hands together, the only sign that what she was saying made her uncomfortable.

Lizzie blinked. "Attacked?" That could mean a lot of things. Pushed, slapped, punched—though none of those options matched the ladylike woman standing before her. Maybe it had been worse? More along the lines of seriously injured, maimed...killed?

"One of the security staff," Harrington said.

"He's fine," Ewan added. "It was one of my clan."

The breath Lizzie had unknowingly held as soon as talk of an attack began whooshed out of her lungs. That was good news. The dragons in Ewan's clan were hard to hurt, and Lizzie didn't see a frail woman making much of a dent in one of those scaly, fire-breathing guys.

Matylda said, "I injured him."

"Oh." Lizzie's dismay leaked into that one word more obviously than she'd have liked. Matylda looked— sounded—so coherent, so rational. So human. "But you're better now."

"Perhaps. Ewan or one of his staff will keep me company for so long as I remain in this condition." Matylda made a moue of distaste. Over the added security or her condition? "What we need to know, and quickly now that introductions have been completed, is what you did to hasten the spread of the magic."

"Ah." Where to start? The multiple sensing wards?

Turning the main lights back on? "Well, we did turn the lights on, but that can't possibly—"

"No," Harrington said. "What type of magic did you do? Did you touch the book? Or try something...unusual?"

Lizzie was known for being rather creative in the magic department. It usually served her well, but even she—as new to magic as she was—knew better than to chuck some newfangled mojo at a dangerous black magic book. "No, of course not. I did cast three—"

"Four," Pilar corrected.

"Right. Four sensing wards in a pretty short window of time." Lizzie wrinkled her nose. "In retrospect, maybe not so clever?"

"Maybe not so clever," Harrington agreed with a mildly censorious look directed at Pilar.

"She's not my keeper," Lizzie said, "so stop it."

Harrington didn't get a chance to reply, because his phone rang. He frowned, clearly considering not answering it, but picked it up. "Max. How can I help you?" Polite, but the tone was frosty.

He listened and then turned away. His voice low and urgent, he asked, "Are you armed?"

The hairs stood up on Lizzie's arms.

"Can you retreat?" Harrington paused. "Shoot it." He turned to Ewan with a grim look. "Shoot it again. I'm sending Ewan." Turning to Lizzie, he added, "And Lizzie." He kept the phone to his ear but covered the mouthpiece. "Lizzie, Ewan, the courtyard, now. The effects of the book have spread to the courtyard. A Lycan in wolf form has cornered Max."

Matylda had damaged a dragon. Lizzie didn't like to think what kind of damage a zombified Lycan to do to a human. Except she did think about it, and the adrenaline hit a millisecond later.

"Shit," Lizzie said as she spun on the ball of her foot and took off at a sprint behind Ewan.

He was faster. Much faster. He wasn't human, and preternatural speed seemed to go hand in hand with shifters' other gifts.

Vivid images of Max facing off against a zombified Lycan wolf lent her some additional speed, but not dragon speed. There was enough time for her to panic on more than one level before arriving. What pack did the wolf belong to? Would John be placed in danger by her actions today?

Ever since she'd joined the Lycan world, she'd been much too immersed in its tangled politics. If they had to kill this wolf, would it cause a war? If he'd already been dead, were they really "killing" him? But that thought faded in the wake of a much more disturbing one: *could* they kill him?

But then she pivoted back to Max. God, Max... Would Max still be standing when they arrived? What would she tell Kenna if Max was injured or worse? He was one of her best friends, her unborn child's father, and quite possibly the love of her life (if she'd ever pack up the last of her failed marriage baggage).

Max was Kenna's John.

A rush of panicky adrenaline took Lizzie the last few feet and through the door to the courtyard.

She didn't know what to expect from an undead wolf

that wasn't a wolf at all but Lycan. Confused, violent, and...?

What she found had her stuttering to a halt.

A crazed wolf's muzzle foamed. Blood and saliva mingled to create a sickly cotton-candy color. Flecks of spittle dotted its darkly matted chest fur and forelegs. Matted with Max's blood? Kenna's?

Max was close, too close to the snapping jaws of the beast.

Kenna... Lizzie jerked her head away from the wolf to find her friend only feet away, bloodied but alive.

Lizzie turned to the wolf, ready to—what, bind it? They couldn't kill the thing. But then she saw the improvised hobble around the wolf's hind legs. Her heart stuttered in her chest and then resumed its frantic pace.

Even partially contained, the wolf was still a terrible hazard.

And Kenna was feet from it. What the hell was she doing here?

Get the pregnant woman away from the scary wolf.

Lizzie rushed to her friend's side and grabbed her elbow. With a solid yank, she pulled Kenna to her feet. "Kenna," Lizzie called, but in vain.

Kenna's huge, dilated eyes didn't blink or shift. All of her attention was focused on the wolf.

Lizzie shook her hard. "Kenna. Inside, now."

Ewan was manhandling the creature into some form of submission when the unthinkable happened: the bound wolf began to burn.

Brilliant flames engulfed him, and waves of heat pulsed through the courtyard. Ewan pulled away unmarked. Dragons didn't burn easily, but the wolf... The wolf burned.

Waves of heat washed over Lizzie, the light seared her retina—and she did nothing.

Her brain couldn't quite manage to process that what was unfolding in front of her. Her world turned dull and muffled, the only light that of the flashing flames.

Two seconds, three, she stood there, caught in her own disbelief. Slowly, the filters her mind had erected fell away. She heard the screams first. Then came the smell.

The terrified, tortured shrieks pulled at her gut, twisting and turning it. Or perhaps it was the acrid scent of burning hair and flesh. She swallowed quickly, trying not to retch.

She wrangled control of her stomach then spun in a circle. There had to be an answer, a solution, something to stop the fire.

She spun around twice before landing on her friend.

Her fire witch friend. It had taken that long for the pieces to fall together. She chalked it up to shock. Watching, smelling, hearing a creature burn and regenerate in an unending circle could do that to a girl. She pressed her hand hard against her stomach. She would not puke.

Kenna, newly awakened to her fire witch powers, had set the undead creature alight with magical fire. How? She had barely lit a candle this morning. Her fear must have enhanced her power, removed her control, triggered some reservoir of power.

One horrific problem loomed: the wolf couldn't be killed. It was already dead. Unless... Was this the answer to IPPC's undead problem? Could fire, more specifically cremation, be the solution?

But as those thoughts flew through Lizzie's mind, the animal's tortured wails continued. It burned...and regenerated and burned and kept burning. It seemed there was no end in sight to its magical store. Whatever had fueled the creature's reanimation kept on ticking, at least enough for it to repair the burn wounds. That poor, frightened animal.

Lizzie clenched Kenna's arm and lost the battle to still her stomach's rioting protests. Acidic bile burned her throat as she retched. She pinched her nose, cupped her mouth, and refused to be caught in this terrible moment.

Ewan was busy tending to Max; she needed to sort this shit out *now*.

Except she needed Kenna to fix it. Kenna had started the fire; she needed to put the flames out.

Lizzie twisted Kenna's arm, trying her damnedest to block out the terrible sounds the animal was making and get her friend's attention.

In her peripheral vision, she could see that the creature regenerated just enough to maintain its wolfish form, certainly enough to fuel the fire, because the flames continued to flare brightly in the corner of her eye and the stench of charred hair and flesh saturated the air.

The damned necromantic magic was keeping pace with Kenna's fire, neither extinguishing the flames nor letting it run its course. If there was a living being behind these actions and not just a little black book of nasty, he or she was a sick bastard. What was to be gained from this horror show?

Lizzie shook Kenna's arm hard and moved to stand in front of her. "Kenna!"

Finally, Kenna blinked. Then her eyes widened. What little color remained drained from her face as she stared over Lizzie's shoulder and watched the tortured, shrieking creature. She started to tremble and then shake violently.

"Kenna." Lizzie placed a hand on either side of Kenna's face, covering her ears. She could feel the dampness of tears on her own cheeks. Her friend needed to get it together and end the animal's suffering.

Except it wasn't an animal. *He* wasn't an animal. He was Lycan, like John. Locked in the body of that wolf was a man. But thinking that was going to make Lizzie lose her shit.

Kenna kept staring at the flames, but she wasn't *doing* anything. She wasn't stopping it.

Lizzie dodged to continue blocking Kenna's persistent gaze. "You have to stop the fire. That thing—it can't die." She pressed her hands hard against either side of Kenna's face and forced their eyes to meet. "Listen to me. Listen! You have to stop it. He'll keep burning. He won't die."

Kenna shook her head, confused.

Lizzie pushed her face closer to Kenna's. "It will keep burning and living. You have to stop the fire."

But Kenna just shook her head.

"Kenna. Look at me. Can you try?"

Kenna's reply was faint, and Lizzie had to strain to hear. "I can't." Kenna's lips trembled, and she said it again, stronger, louder. "I can't stop it."

"Yes. Yes, you can," Lizzie yelled. Because if Kenna would just hear her, she'd try.

"A fire extinguisher." Kenna gasped. "Just like"—she hiccupped and struggled for breath—"just like any fire... Lizzie, I didn't mean—"

A fire extinguisher? If that was the only choice, then Lizzie would damned well find a fire extinguisher. She ran back to the house. As she flew by the wolf, she saw Ewan rolling on the ground with him, trying to smother the flames.

Thank goodness for dragons and their affinity for fire.

Forty-five more seconds. The wolf—the Lycan—burned for forty-five seconds.

Lizzie knew because Kenna told her. After Lizzie had separated Ewan from the beast. After the wolf had been drenched in foam. That was all her friend kept saying. That she'd counted. That it had been forty-five seconds.

Lizzie didn't have time to deal with a shell-shocked Kenna, not immediately. She had to get medical care for Max, who had a serious injury to his arm and was still bleeding profusely despite Ewan's attempts to stanch the flow.

It had been Max's blood that coated the Lycan's fur, not Kenna's. So as Kenna continued to mutter, Lizzie had to leave her for the more seriously wounded.

Once Frank, their resident healer, had carted Max off to the infirmary, securing the wolf more permanently became a priority. Lizzie checked in with Kenna again, and while she was no worse, she was also no better. Lizzie had to get the wolf secured, so she could lend some much-needed comfort to her friend.

The only truly secure room was located in the base-ment, closer to the book. Not gonna happen. Stashing a violent undead creature within close proximity to the book that had brought him back to life was begging for trouble.

Ewan and Tavish, one of his security team, had muzzled the wolf and were restraining him.

Tavish frowned. "Transport is always risky, and if he escapes—"

"Wait," Lizzie said as she approached the two men. She didn't get too close, because even a muzzled Lycan locked in some kind of wrestling hold by two human-form dragons was treacherous. "You can't be thinking of loading him up and driving him out of here. What about contagion?"

Which then brought Max front and center, because he'd suffered deep tissue damage from a Lycan bite. If zombie-ism was catching, then Max was about to face some serious life changes.

A weak, panicked laugh escaped before Lizzie could swallow it back. Life changes, right? Great way to frame Max's personal crisis. A possible zombie infection and looming parenthood seemed to be all scrambled together in her brain. Not funny.

"Calm down and take a breath," Ewan said.

Lizzie blinked. Was he talking to her? She was the queen of crises, having survived far worse than the little skirmish she'd just witnessed. Heck, she hadn't even been in danger of getting zapped into another plane of exis-tence or torn apart by unfriendly wolves. She had a handle on the situation. She had to.

Ewan refrained from rolling his eyes, but Lizzie could see exasperation flicker across his face. She knew that look all too well—and the dragons claimed they didn't have much in common with Lycan.

"It's not contagious, Lizzie. It's magic." Ewan shook his head. "We do need a secure destination, though. We're not sure if simply removing him from proximity to the book will be enough, or if there's a time component."

"You think once the dead are made undead, they've got magic stored?" She gave him an uncertain look before adding, "Like a battery?"

"Any chance you guys can argue about this while we drive around the block?" Tavish asked. "Because I'm thinking that's the fastest way to test the proximity versus battery-operated theory."

"Battery-operated?" Lizzie snorted. She had to be punch-drunk tired to find that funny. To find anything funny at this point. Although she had just laughed hysterically about Max possibly being infected by a zombie bite. She wasn't herself.

The zombified Lycan had been roasting only minutes previous. Humor shouldn't be anywhere near the four of them, although it helped that any visible evidence of the ordeal had vanished. The wolf's skin and fur had completely regenerated.

As she inspected him, Lizzie made eye contact. What she saw, or rather *didn't* see, sobered her instantly.

"No one's home," she whispered.

"Right, I'm taking Sparky here to the car," Tavish said. "Someone get the door for me."

Ewan relinquished control to Tavish and then opened

the door. As he waited for his second-in-command to haul the surprisingly subdued wolf inside, he said, "Unlike your great-aunt, when his body regenerated, there was no consciousness to fill it. He's all survival and instinct at this point. If Frank hadn't sedated him, I'm guessing he'd still be trying to disembowel us or rip our throats out."

On that disturbing note, Ewan tugged the door shut behind him.

With the wolf temporarily managed and Max in the infirmary, Lizzie turned her attention to Kenna.

Kenna had been present for everything—the restraining of the wolf, carting Max off to the infirmary, the dragons discussing the Lycan's containment—but she'd barely moved. Roasting an (almost) living creature and watching it burn could push a girl into a state of shock.

Lizzie noted her own shaking hands. She was more accustomed than Kenna to the adrenaline ride of living in the magic-using community, and she was struggling.

Another of Ewan's security men came through the door and made a final pass of the courtyard. Not a bad idea, considering the book's reach had extended this far. Maybe they could catch the next zombified creature before it got the jump on one of them. Lizzie didn't doubt that there would be another.

She watched with a keen eye, ready to...help? Flee in the opposite direction? Make sure Kenna was nowhere near so she wouldn't light another creature on fire? She wasn't sure, and she didn't find out. The courtyard was clear.

As the guard passed by Kenna, she emerged from her stupor and called out frantically, "Where's Max? Where did you take him?"

"Infirmary." He gave her a critical look. "Where you should be headed. First floor. Second floor, American. Do you need help?"

Kenna shook her head, but Lizzie said, "Yes, she needs help. I'll take her." She carefully placed an arm around Kenna's shoulders, trying not to startle her. "You're in shock. That's why everything seems so strange and you're having a hard time thinking straight." And why Max had been carted away without her even realizing it.

Kenna nodded, but her face still had the same blank look.

Gently guiding her into the house and down the hall, Lizzie gave Kenna just enough information to answer her most immediate questions but skipped the gory details and minimized what was looking to be much more than just *bug*pocalypse.

For the next half-hour, Lizzie made certain Kenna and Max were recovering—assisted by some healer magic, naturally.

But then everything post-crisis-related was handled and she had a moment to think.

Relief. That was what hit her first. Knee-wobbling, head-swimming relief. Max and Kenna would be fine. Kenna's baby, also fine. And no other dead-and-alive-again creatures had cropped up.

That they knew of.

Yet.

There would be more zombies. How could there not? The book hadn't been stopped. Just because they couldn't see its nasty magical tendrils reaching out and flipping undead switches willy-nilly didn't mean it wasn't happening.

Which was when the fear and frustration struck. What would be next? How would they stop it? What if it was something worse than a Lycan? Something stronger than a handful of dragons? Something Ewan and his men couldn't subdue?

Yeah, that needed to not happen. Which meant Lizzie needed to get off her butt and sort this problem out. She didn't have time to dither. Because zombies. Because Gwen.

And, dammit, she missed John.

She retrieved her phone from her back pocket and checked for messages.

Nothing from John. She couldn't blame him. He was busy sorting out their lives—their future—and that required an investment of time and focused attention on the Texas pack.

And she'd heard nothing from Ewan. Either their wolf's zombified state had persisted further than a quick spin around the block, or Ewan had been caught in an awkward situation.

According to Max's recounting of events as he'd been stitched up, the wolf had re-formed from buried skeletal remains. She didn't even want to know the particulars of how a Lycan ended up buried in the library's private courtyard. Harrington was no idiot, so Lizzie knew the body predated IPPC's occupancy of the building. That wasn't the pressing question, however.

If the necromantic magic faded, Ewan would be left with the remains of the Lycan. Which meant he was either carting around a very large, very angry wild animal in the back of his vehicle or a pile of bones. Neither would look particularly good during a traffic stop.

She smacked her head. "Please, please let the dragons carting the demented, undead wolf not be stopped by the local police."

She added one more "please" for good measure, and then she waited.

5

<hr>

Lizzie's patience diminished proportionately to the quantity of caffeine she consumed. Since she'd consumed several cups, waiting for Ewan, Tavish, and their new pet to return was excruciating.

Time to head to the kitchen for a proper meal. Bacon made everything better.

She was only feet away from the answer to her culinary prayers when the troublesome awareness of her location resurfaced. She was in Prague, and as awesome as fried strips of pork fat were, not every country appreciated its genius.

Imagine her surprise when she strolled into the kitchen to find that they'd stocked American bacon—just for her.

"Harrington?" she asked.

The chef smiled and then busied himself preparing the BLT she'd requested. "No. A Mr. Braxton had a package delivered special for you."

John. Her heart did a little rat-a-tat-tat. She loved that guy. He was considerate in all the little ways, if arranging for a specialty meat delivery was little. He also knew she could get a little cranky when she was hungry, and that she did love her bacon.

"I'll make a tray for you? Or would you prefer to eat in the dining room?"

Lizzie took that to mean "get out of my kitchen, crazy fried-fat-eating lady." She thanked him and agreed that a tray would be great. She edged around the corner in an attempt to remove herself from the chef's domain—he was fulfilling her bizarre American food request, after all—and planted herself against the hallway wall.

She pulled her phone out and checked she hadn't missed an update. Kenna was passed out and recovering from her ordeal for the moment but was supposed to text when she woke. And Ewan—well, Lizzie still wasn't entirely certain he hadn't been locked up for crimes against wildlife.

Her phone pinged with a text. Ewan. She hoped for good news as she opened the text.

No, we have not been stopped by the authorities. How foolish do you think us?

She'd been a little impatient, so she might have texted a few less-than-probable scenarios as she'd waited to hear from them. His fault for taking so long to get back to her. Despite his snarky tone, she was thankful Ewan hadn't been forced to explain the reason he was carting an oversized wolf around the good people of Prague.

Her phone pinged again with a second message.

The Lycan remains undead.

Well, hell. She quickly replied asking how far they'd driven.

As she waited for a reply, she couldn't help pondering the stash of equipment a dragon might have handy in his SUV.

Lizzie snorted. Knowing how prepared Lycan were, it wouldn't surprise her if dragons were the same and Ewan had a tarp or three stashed in his vehicle. Much as the two groups hated to admit it, they had a lot in common.

Too far.

Too far—what did that even mean? She called Ewan, but it rolled to voicemail immediately. Looked like she was out of the loop until Ewan deigned to fill her in.

To be fair, if he had any useful information, she was sure he'd share it. But that didn't help her frustration. And she was hungry, dammit.

Except her empty stomach wasn't the real issue. No, the real issue was Gwen.

Lizzie had been trying to juggle the undead problem and Gwen's kidnapping, but all she'd managed was to deal with a few dead bugs, *make* a few more undead bugs (oops), put out a fire that never should have started in the first place, and flit between Kenna and Harrington hoping for some more information.

Splitting her attention had accomplished less than nothing. Not only had she made no headway on either crisis, but her priorities felt all sorts of jumbled up.

Her heart was with Kenna and Gwen. But to help Gwen, Lizzie had to help Harrington. And to help Harrington, she had to figure out how to kill some undead stuff—not just bugs, apparently—and keep the wicked book from the super-secret library room from spreading its nasty undead magic.

Soulless zombies acting only on instinct were bad news. Making sure they didn't start cruising around town, thereby risking a reveal scare and injuring people, was an important task. People, possibly many people, might die if she didn't find an off switch for the necromancy book. Unfortunately, the importance of the task didn't change where her heart lay.

She wanted to hunt down some nasty Coven of Light witches and rescue Gwen.

And now Lizzie was thinking like a psychotic toddler. Mean and lacking in impulse control.

One rampaging zombie Lycan in wolf form could easily kill a dozen people. And what if a dragon corpse was stashed within the book's zapping range? Or something else equally dangerous?

She rubbed her eyes. Not shockingly, they were dry and gritty. Moral support, that was what she needed right now. And some sleep, but she'd have to make do with a pep talk.

She pulled her phone out and called John.

"Hey, you okay?" His deep voice hit her in all the right spots. No, not the pervy ones. She was too keyed up for that. It calmed her agitated nerves and soothed her aching heart. She knew she'd been missing him, but she hadn't realized quite how much.

"I am now."

"What's going on?" He sounded casual enough, but she knew what was going through that wolfy head of his. He wanted to be with her—that was a given—but if she let on how conflicted and stressed and over-caffeinated she was, he'd only feel worse about not being here. If he knew she was struggling, the distance between them and the commitments that kept him in Texas would twist him up in knots.

He'd want to be here to make everything better, or at least hold her if he couldn't, and since she wanted those things too, she'd have to be extra careful.

Striving for a light tone, she said, "I can't just call because I miss you?"

His rumbling laughter might have hit her in those *other* right spots. If she wasn't completely focused on her case. Which she was. Totally.

His laughter died, and, in an intimate tone, he said, "Missing you, too." He cleared his throat. "Now, why are you really calling?"

"Moral conundrum."

"Okay. I'll give it my best shot."

They didn't always see eye to eye on moral questions. Lizzie tended to be a rule follower, and John...wasn't.

As the Alpha of the Texas Pack, he followed Lycan laws—the ones he had to—but Lizzie had been raised in the human world with human laws, and John was much less likely to be compliant with human laws that conflicted with his moral code.

None of that really mattered, though, because John got her—intimately, deeply, on all levels.

"Two trains, two tracks, both racing toward a collision but in opposite directions from one another. You can prevent one crash, maybe, but probably not both. One train has a single passenger, someone who's important to you. The other train has several passengers, but they're all strangers." Lizzie considered the IPPC staff, all in close proximity to the book and not planning to evacuate anytime soon, and all an incredible group of dedicated and gifted individuals. "Scratch that. The second train's passengers are greater in number and definitely really cool people."

"Your equation's left out a few of the variables."

She shrugged, then realized he couldn't see her. "Yeah, but I think you get the major issues."

"Of course. And if you're going to ask what I'd do? If the coven had you, there's nothing that would keep me from getting you back. No pack business, no secondary crisis." He sighed. "But you're not me, and that wouldn't necessarily be *your* right decision."

True, she wasn't him, but they weren't so different.

In her heart of hearts, she knew if John had been the one captured, nothing could keep her away. Not a commitment to Harrington or IPPC, not the low probability of a successful outcome, not even hell's hounds nipping at her feet.

Yeah, she'd be super dead if John was being held captive.

Then again, there was always Kenna and the pack. They'd do their best to make sure Lizzie didn't jump off a cliff without a parachute.

A frustrated groan slipped past her lips, and immediately she regretted it. The distance between them was the knife, and she shouldn't twist it.

A rumbling on the opposite end of the line answered. "I hate that I can't be there."

"I know." Regret chewed at her stomach—or maybe that was plain old hunger. Where the hell was that BLT? She shook her head. "When I called, I mostly just wanted to hear your voice. I've got this under control. Really."

"Uh-huh." His voice lowered to a rough whisper. "I love you. Keep yourself safe."

"Yeah, back at you, Fluffy."

She hung up on his sharp bark of laughter.

6

———

Lizzie got her BLT.

It was perfect: crisply fried bacon offset by a flavorful heirloom tomato and fresh, leafy lettuce with just a dab of mayo, all between two thick slices of freshly baked bread.

And she even had the dining area to herself, so she could enjoy it in blissful, crisis-free silence.

Naturally, Ewan texted just as she sank her teeth into the nearly orgasmic first bite of that oh-so-perfect culinary work of art.

She chewed as she read his text.

Just pulled up. No joy with the wolf.

That dragon knew how to spoil a good sandwich. She'd have to finish in three minutes or less. That was how long it would take Ewan to get into the house and crash her meal.

She tried for proactive and replied by text between bites: *Where am I meeting you?*

But he was fleeter of foot than she'd credited him with. He walked into the dining room and replied, "Here."

A girl had to eat. She took another bite and stared at him, waiting for the recap.

"I've got my men securing the Lycan in one of the basement additions."

She kept chewing and raised her eyebrows.

Ewan, clever man, got the hint. He sat down across from her. "We drove the perimeter of the city and saw no change. Since we don't have a secure offsite location to store him—"

"To gauge how long it would take for his battery to die." She eyed the fizzy water the kitchen staff had provided and shrugged. She chugged half the glass. She wouldn't mention the fact that the basement was less than ideal for so many reasons. Ewan knew that, so it had to be the least of all evils.

"Right, if the magic even works that way. For all we know, there's some form of inertia that comes into play. Once these dead creatures are reanimated, they could stay that way until something flips the off switch."

"You really think that's a possibility?" It was a much more disturbing one than the previous hypotheses: a magical battery that exhausted itself, or a specific geographic reach for the book. At least their previous theories meant the creatures would self-terminate. At some as-yet-to-be-discovered point, but still, there was an end in sight.

"I don't know. I need you to have a look at him. Now

that we've verified we don't have an easy way to shut him down, we're going to use him as a test subject."

The last bite of her sandwich stuck in her throat. She chugged the remainder of her water, but it didn't help. He just had to go and ruin her meal by mentioning torture. Testing, torture...tomato, tomahto.

She cleared her throat. "I'm not sure I'm comfortable with that." She swallowed past the thickening lump of guilt. "He was alive once. For all we know, he could still have family and friends."

Okay, that wasn't very likely, but it just seemed wrong to use a Lycan as a lab rat.

Ewan crossed his arms. It made him look buff (which he was) and intimidating (which he also was, to some people). But she was an Alpha's mate. That crap didn't work on her.

She crossed *her* arms and met him frown for frown. "Experimentation on a creature that's just one step shy of alive exceeds my ethical boundaries."

"One step shy?" He quirked an eyebrow. "Unlike Matylda, this Lycan has no soul. He's an empty vessel, pulled from one moment to the next by nothing more than the basest of his instincts."

A shiver crawled up her spine. Was that what a ghost was? A person's soul? She'd never thought about ghosts in those terms. Didn't *want* to think about them that way.

And she really didn't want to think about the shell of her body cruising around without her most important parts—the parts that made her human, the parts that made her a unique individual.

"If you're done?" Ewan indicated the plate she'd practically licked clean.

She shoved her chair away from the table but stopped at the side table for coffee before following him down the hall to the basement stairs. Thank goodness for to-go cups, or she'd probably have skipped it—and she really needed that boost about now.

The idea of using the captured Lycan as nothing more than a guinea pig made her stomach do flips. Caffeine wouldn't help, but she needed the biggest of all pick-me-ups right now.

It was some small consolation that the Lycan was trapped in its wolf form. Bad enough to magically poke and prod a wolf that was so much more than a wolf. If their test subject had a human face, she really didn't think she could do it.

"Wait a second." She stopped so suddenly on the basement stairs that she splattered coffee on her shirt. "Why aren't we using the bugs?"

Ewan didn't pretend to understand. He shook his head and gave her the look. The one that men the world over had mastered. It was about as clear as if he'd said, "What the hell are you smoking, little woman?"

Then Ewan's eyes crinkled, and he said, "I would never say such a thing. And you should think more quietly."

"Crap." She'd forgotten about dragons' telepathy trick. And this wasn't the first time she'd been told she thought louder than a cheerleader screaming through a bullhorn. "Anyway—bugs? Can't we use them as test subjects? They don't even come close to showing up on my ethical radar, wrong though that may be."

"Won't work, not unless you're familiar with bug language and behavior." He gestured for her to precede him down the last few steps.

"Bugs have their own language?"

Ewan sighed. "I haven't a clue."

As they approached the door to the containment room, Lizzie steeled herself to enter. She prepared herself to see the Lycan, and even though she knew he was recovered, images of his burning flesh and the stink of charred hair assailed her.

Ewan opened the door to reveal a wolf with intact flesh and fur and a mad look in his eye. It was that look that made Lizzie thankful for the chains wrapped securely around him. "Why haven't you drugged him again?"

"Frank tried. The drugs didn't work a second time. We'll just have to restrain him. He doesn't feel pain in the same way a fully alive creature does. He reacts to it, but he doesn't experience it beyond the immediate moment."

That might be true, but it didn't help.

"All right. Let's get this started. Standing around watching him cut himself on the chains isn't going to make me feel any better about this," Lizzie said. "We know fire won't harm him. Bullets and physical trauma are equally ineffective. What's left?"

Ewan blinked. "I thought we'd start with a sensing ward."

Oh. And now she felt like a complete monster. Non-invasive measures were definitely the place to start.

She went through the steps of gathering her magic, formulating her intent, then applying will. Unlike during her rocky beginnings with magic, she flowed through steps in seconds these days.

She cast a sparkly net of finely woven magic and let it settle on the wolf. He shouldn't have felt a thing. Sensing wards were quiet magic, even subtle when more sophisticated casters employed them. (Lizzie was rarely subtle.) But even the loudest, brightest, flashiest of sensing wards weren't typically detectable by the subject. They certainly didn't harm the subject.

The shriek of an injured animal pierced her ears, and as quickly as she'd cast the ward, she dissolved it.

"What. The. Fuck." Tavish's statement hung in the now-silent air.

Lizzie had no answer. Sensing wards didn't harm, and they didn't cause pain. That was pretty basic, magic 101 or 102 stuff.

She circled the wolf and examined him—without the aid of magic.

He'd ceased struggling against the chains. His breath came in short, sharp, panting breaths, and his head hung low.

He looked exhausted. Worn out from his struggles and the pain.

"Thoughts?" Ewan asked, drilling her with a probing look.

"That shouldn't have happened." She replayed in her mind's eye the brief moment between casting and dissolving the ward. There'd been something. She'd barely glimpsed it, but only because she'd been focused on ending the wolf's pain. Her ward had picked up magic that had flared strong and bright.

"Do it again." Ewan must have seen her discomfort, because he reminded her, "It has no memory, and I know you detected something."

He was right, and so she cast again. This time, she was ready. She didn't take time to settle in to the feel of her magic as it worked. She cast, and then reeled in the data. Her focus narrowed to the sliver of magic that was other, and she took a snapshot—the look, the feel, the taste of it —then shut down the ward.

"You found something," Ewan said, but she needed a moment to think.

She held up her hand, asking him silently to give her some space. Closing her eyes, she took out the memory she'd created and turned it around in her head. Some-thing about it felt familiar. It was on the tip of her tongue, the edge of her mind. So close…

"Oh, shit." Lizzie looked at the two men as she pulled out her phone. As she waited for Harrington to answer, she said, "Elin. You need to find Elin."

7

———

Elin was nowhere to be found.

Lizzie sat across from Harrington in his office and listened as Ewan and Tavish reported on their search of the house. When they finished, she stifled her fifth or sixth yawn.

"If she's in the wind," Lizzie said, "then maybe we're in the clear."

"She's not in the wind. She's simply yet to be discovered," Harrington clarified. "I suspect she's still on the property."

"Agreed." Ewan stood at attention, looking especially stern and forbidding. Failure didn't agree with him. "She did this for a reason, and until her motivation is uncovered, we can only assume her plan is as yet incomplete."

"Tell me again what you saw, Lizzie." Harrington poured himself a whiskey without offering the others a glass.

"It was brief, but I'm certain the magic I felt was Elin's,

and I'm almost as certain she didn't fuel the Lycan's reanimation. Her magic acted as a shield and masked any other traces of magic."

"Your men are working on a deeper look at Elin's background?" Harrington asked Ewan, who nodded in reply.

A knock at the door was followed by Matylda's entrance. Another of Ewan's staff escorted her through the door, then disappeared after Ewan dismissed him.

Harrington studied Matylda with a grim look. "I understand you want to have a look at the Lycan."

That was news to Lizzie.

"No. I requested an opportunity to observe Lizzie cast her sensing ward so I might evaluate the results myself."

Also news to Lizzie, but she had one obvious objection. "My ward actually hurt him. It interacted with Elin's shield in a way I don't understand, but it definitely causes him pain."

Matylda's eyes narrowed. "If I'm correct, it is not a *shield* that surrounds this Lycan. I need to observe the effects of the ward before I can say with certainty, but I believe I know who is behind the misuse of the necromancy book."

"But we know who it is," Lizzie said. "We can't *find* her, but her identity is no secret."

"You don't know, child. You don't have the slightest inkling." Matylda's gaze softened, and Lizzie suspected she saw a hint of pity there.

Her aunt's pronouncement was vague enough to spark Lizzie's curiosity. But Harrington, being the suspicious sort, asked, "Why should I trust you, when you refuse to disclose relevant information?"

"Because I'm the only one who knows what we're dealing with," Matylda replied evenly.

"*What* we're dealing with?" Ewan asked. "You're saying that the sixteen-year old Norwegian intern that we background checked isn't a spell caster?"

"A spell caster, a witch, Lycan. If she's who I suspect, then she is all of these and none."

"I trust her," Lizzie said. "And didn't you tell me, Ewan, that the Lycan retains no memory of any pain he suffers?" Not that the wolf's failure to recall made inflicting pain less morally questionable, but Lizzie trusted her gut, and her gut told her to trust Matylda. "Come on. Let's do this."

Except when Lizzie got up and headed to the door, no one followed her, not even Matylda.

A few erratic heartbeats passed before Harrington relented and agreed...and then everyone filed out.

Four minutes later, they had their answer.

Piled into the room with the chained Lycan, Lizzie cast her ward. She'd warned Matylda to be fast, and the agreed-upon signal (a tap to the shoulder) was almost instantaneous. Lizzie untangled the ward she'd cast, and then waited for the verdict.

"It's her." Matylda cast a pitying look on the wolf and then left the room. Ewan and Tavish were right behind, since her minder had left earlier.

Harrington didn't say a word as he held the door for Lizzie.

She figured they would tramp back up to Harrington's

office, but Matylda made a beeline for the library, also located in the basement.

When Lizzie and Harrington entered the room, she already had a book pulled from the shelf. She pointed at it and said, "Nymphs."

"A nymph?" If Ewan had ears, they'd be perking up. "Are you sure?"

Matylda nodded and pointed at the book. Lizzie took the hint and cast a ward. She found her magic, formed the question—which was simple, since Matylda hadn't give her any information—and applied will.

The result was...unexpected.

Words poured from the book. Lizzie had never encountered a warded book so eager to let loose its secrets. She had to concentrate to slow the stream, but when she did, the words became sentences, and then they became a story.

The first story was heartbreaking, the second no better, and the third made her eyes well. By the fourth, she'd become so entangled that it took her several seconds to realize that Harrington was shaking her arm.

She stepped away from the book, as if physical distance would limit the pull of the words. She took a deep breath. "Okay, I got a glimpse into the lives of four young girls." She took another breath. "Four teenage girls who were possessed, their lives stolen, their power appropriated and used for foul purposes, and then their physical bodies discarded. I don't know what happened to their non-physical selves."

"Their souls," Matylda said. "I'll spare you the knowledge, but know that nothing good comes when a nymph possesses a body."

"I thought they'd been eradicated." Ewan looked at Tavish for confirmation, and he nodded his agreement.

"Apparently not," Matylda said.

"This one certainly isn't quiet." Harrington paused then swore. "Ewan, you need to have your staff check on Emme, Elin's aunt. She unexpectedly claimed a few weeks of comp time just as Elin was beginning her internship."

Matylda shook her head. "You should check, but almost certainly she's been eliminated. Anyone who would spot the sudden change in her personality would be. Memories are not a problem. When a nymph possesses a body, she assumes the memories and powers of the host, but personality is another matter."

"How do we kill a nymph?" Lizzie asked.

Matylda turned to Ewan. "Dragon? How does one kill a nymph?"

"Fire, water," he replied. "Earth to contain."

"We drown or burn her? Or bury her and hope no one digs her up?" Lizzie's eyes burned. *Too soon* didn't begin to describe her feelings on dealing with fire of any kind, let alone cremating a person. Even if the person in question was an evil nymph bent on reanimating all of the corpses in Prague. Which raised the question: "Why? Why is Elin, or whatever her name really is, doing this?"

"Power," Ewan and Matylda said, one on top of the other.

Matylda inclined her head, indicating that Ewan should explain.

"Nymphs have always been seekers of power," he said. "Human history paints them as carefree, playful women. Always beautiful and tied to nature in some way. While their origin is unknown, they did at one point prey upon women who collected water from community springs, which could explain their historic tie to nature. But they were never benign. History has bathed them in an unearned positive light."

"They hunted much as a lion lying in wait for a parched water buffalo would," Matylda added. "They are most certainly not benign."

At this point, Harrington's silence ended and he began to drill Matylda. Much more his style than watching from the sidelines. "Why here and now? How did she learn of the necromancy book? What advantage is there to her in reanimating these corpses? How is she powering the reanimations? And what magic has she used on the Lycan?"

And then he waited. Lizzie knew he expected answers to these questions, quite possibly in the order he'd asked them. They weren't rhetorical or a way to organize his thoughts. His thoughts were perfectly organized at all times—so far as she could tell.

"The ward Lizzie triggered wasn't protection," Matylda said. "It's an insidious combination of ward, spell, and the subject's magic. It grows stronger the longer it remains active, pulling increasing amounts of energy from the subject."

"And the purpose?" Harrington asked.

"Control over the subject. She makes them her puppets." Matylda straightened her spine and lifted her chin. "As to why now, I can only assume she plans to use the book to create her own army of soldiers for some unsavory, objectionable purpose."

Mind control scared the snot out of Lizzie. Losing control of her own body... She shivered. "Why aren't you affected?"

"The soulless are the easiest targets. It requires less effort on her part to cast, weave, and bind this hybrid magic of hers to an empty shell."

Lizzie nodded. "If she's trying to control potentially hundreds, she'd pick the easiest."

"I've heard of nymphs stealing bodies and their magic," Ewan said. "But not retaining magic from one body to the next. And combining magic? That's a precursor to Big Magic. Should we be concerned that she's employing Big Magic?"

The look on Harrington and Tavish's faces when Ewan mentioned Big Magic would have been comical if they were anyone else. But seeing two men as powerful as them flinch at the mere mention of it wigged Lizzie out.

She was familiar with the concept. When the sum was greater than the parts contributed, that was Big Magic. The name came from the exponentially greater amount of magical power generated. It was scary stuff, the magical equivalent of going nuclear.

Lizzie swallowed a yawn, then cleared her throat. "So no Big Magic? Just to clarify."

"No," Harrington said. "I don't see how she could mask that. But if it's not Big Magic, what's powering the re-animations? We're not picking up traces of death magic either."

"That is the question." Grimly, Ewan said, "If we find Elin, I'll be sure to ask."

"And we're sure she's still here?" Lizzie couldn't help wonder if Elin had detected which way the wind was blowing. Matylda's reanimation hadn't gone to plan. She was an old soul with a great deal of knowledge. If Elin knew much about Matylda, she might be worried that Matylda's newly corporeal—and vocal—existence would be a problem for her. Then her attempt to control Matylda had failed. "Maybe she's running? Giving up on a failing plan?"

No one replied, but one look around the room told Lizzie all she needed to know. She was alone in her hope.

Unfortunately, she had a bit of a problem. Stress, adrenaline, and caffeine weren't doing their part to keep Lizzie awake. Her jaw cracked with the yawn she couldn't hold back.

Harrington glanced at his watch. Yes, the man still wore a watch. "Why don't you head to bed, Lizzie? Get some sleep, and we'll reconvene in the morning. In the interim, Ewan and his men will keep looking for Elin and digging in her background."

Lizzie scrubbed a hand across her face. She could barely string her thoughts together, so Harrington was right. She needed some rest before she'd be up to challenging the likes of a nymph-possessed spell caster with the face of an innocent girl.

And sometimes, all a problem needed was a good night's sleep. Fingers crossed that was true in this case.

8

———

Sleep didn't solve any of Lizzie's problems other than providing her with a clearer head. But something exciting happened while she slept: other people kept working, plugging away at the two crises that had consumed Lizzie's every waking moment for two days, and they came up with some pivotal information.

The dragons (long as they'd lived) and Harrington (with as many contacts as he had) had failed to acquire a very specific nugget of knowledge.

Magic communities tended to favor their own and distrust outsiders. They also held their knowledge close. So it wasn't unheard of for each group to have secrets that weren't shared between magic-user types. Lizzie knew very little about dragons, for example.

Witches were an extreme example. They not only believed themselves a class above other magic-users, but there were special groups within their society—like the

Coven of Light—that focused on acquiring and securing knowledge.

In the Coven of Light's case, the pursuit of knowledge trumped other, smaller considerations, like the well-being of humans, free will (witch and human), and life in general. They had no problem murdering left and right to achieve their goals. The Coven of Light made most cults sound like a walk in the park.

But they were exceptional at gathering information.

"Explain to me again what Kenna found." Lizzie sat across the dining table from Harrington. He'd insisted she eat as he updated her on the latest.

"In that book you've both been digging through. You know the one?" He buttered his toast with enviable precision as he waited for Lizzie to confirm.

"The witch's diary?"

He confirmed, but she knew it had to be. She'd had a feeling about that book. The thing had practically tapped her on the shoulder, begging to be read, every time she'd come within spitting distance of it.

"Wellsprings. Naturally occurring magic that gathers and forms a reservoir of magical energy."

Her fork clattered on her plate. "Holy crap. You think that's it. You think there's one here." She retrieved the abandoned utensil and scooped a forkful of fluffy eggs into her mouth. "Wait. Wouldn't Matylda know if her house sat atop the magical equivalent of an untapped oil well?"

Harrington eyed her askance until she closed her mouth, chewed, and swallowed. "I've asked her, and if there is one here, she's unaware of its existence. But she's not the builder of the house."

"Hm. I don't know. The secret chamber where the taboo books were hidden—"

"Matylda's resting place."

"Yes," Lizzie said. "There's no outside access, and to fade into the room, you have to already know the location. The secret was passed down through the family. I can't imagine the builders of the house passed down the secret room's location and not the existence of a magic wellspring."

If Kenna hadn't left town to prep for her mother's recovery mission, Lizzie would have hit her up to pull more information from the witch's diary. Unlike most magic books, the record keeper who'd recorded the witch's diary had made it impossible for another record keeper to single-handedly retrieve information from the book. The combined efforts of both a witch and a spell caster were required.

"I'll verify whether Matylda has any knowledge when our meeting concludes."

Suddenly suspicious, Lizzie asked, "What have you been doing with her while we're sorting out her problem?"

"Her problem?" Harrington raised an eyebrow. "Is that what we're calling an acute case of zombie-ism?" She scowled, and he said, "Calm yourself. She offered to relay what knowledge she could recall of the library books. She's been working with Pilar to make notes for the librarian."

She couldn't help noticing he didn't mention Emme, which worried her.

Lizzie really liked Emme. She'd dedicated significant energy and time to cataloguing the contents of the library and was passionate about the books. Once they managed to pull the library safely through Elin's zombie outbreak crisis, Lizzie would really like to see Emme on the other side of it.

"Ewan has no knowledge of wellsprings, and his people haven't detected the magic to this point. He's relying on us to track and cap its magic."

"I guess that means we're headed back to the dead bug room."

Harrington inclined his head. "Yes, though I thought you might like to finish your breakfast first. You seem more than usually distracted by hunger."

Then he looked at her. For a while.

She chewed and swallowed the last of her English muffin. "What?"

"Is there something you'd like to share?"

Annoying, obnoxious man. Why couldn't he say what he meant?

She finished her tea, but the brief hesitation didn't work to make her less snappish. "I don't know what you mean. If you have a problem, then ask already."

He cleared his throat delicately. "Your temper is shorter, your appetite greater... You've been engaged a few months, mated longer."

She still wasn't getting it. But then suddenly she was, and she laughed. "I'm tired because I've been traveling.

I'm hungry because I stress-eat. I am *not* cooking up a wolf pup in my womb."

Pregnant? No way. They took precautions, so there was no way she was knocked up.

Wait—was there?

There was that one time...

Harrington stood abruptly and cupped her elbow. "You've gone completely white. Are you sure you're well?"

She stared at him as she did a little mental math. "Oh, shit."

Harrington sighed. "You're pregnant."

She denied it immediately. Because she didn't *know* she was. She suspected. Suspecting wasn't knowing. And no way in hell was anyone getting that information before John.

She must have broadcast her thoughts, because Harrington settled down in the chair next to her and very quietly, very calmly said, "We'll call Frank in for a quick examination. He can..." He gestured to her midsection.

Since when was Harrington so squeamish? Didn't the man have kids of his own? Maybe he didn't. She glanced at his ring finger, which was bare. She'd always assumed there was a Mrs. Harrington waiting somewhere in the rolling green hills of England, safe from all the magical baddies and the near-world-ending drama.

"The exam won't take but a moment," Harrington said, pulling her from her musings of a wholly imagined Mrs. Harrington.

"No."

"No?" His reaction floored her. He looked nervous.

"No. The answer won't change our plans." She lifted

her chin. "And you will not be the first person outside of myself and my doctor to find out I'm pregnant."

Harrington tugged at the collar of his shirt, and she had to fight to keep her jaw from dropping. The man was ruffled. Harrington, ruffled. Ever-cool, dispassionate Harrington. He hadn't been anything like this when Kenna had caught the pregnancy bug.

Not that Lizzie had. Because she didn't know—wouldn't know—until after the zombies were squashed and Elin was locked up in nymph-proof cuffs.

John wasn't her only concern. She had very mixed thoughts about having a child so soon in her relationship. But a child, John's child... She was suddenly giddy. She had to swallow a sob; the good—no, the best—kind of tears were imminent. Happiness descended in a wave, and she was overcome with how much she wanted John's child.

Even if it was a little soon. Even if the timing could be better. Even if she had serious concerns about pregnancy and bad-guy-ass-kicking existing within overlapping moments of her life.

But she hadn't lied to Harrington. Her theoretical pregnancy aside, the situation remained otherwise unchanged. Reanimation was still happening—per Harrington over morning tea, the dragons had wrangled both a cat and a bird overnight—and Kenna's mom still needed rescuing, and therefore Harrington's (IPPC's) clout.

"I think we've had enough distraction for the morning." Lizzie pushed her chair away from the table. "Time to use some creative magic to find that wellspring and shut off the tap."

She'd swear she heard Harrington groan when she mentioned creative magic. She smiled.

She might have been hesitant to get creative when she and Pilar had been taking stock earlier, but plain Jane sensing wards had accelerated the effects of the book.

They needed to find and cap the wellspring, so they had to do something innovative. And, really, how much worse could they make it?

9

———

Lizzie liked to think of herself as a glass-half-full kind of person. Right now, she was feeling awfully close to half-empty instead.

She was already tired, and she'd woken up less than hour ago. She'd passed on the coffee she wanted to grab on the way out of the dining room, in case... Well, just in case. Not like she'd been doing research on how knocked up ladies were supposed to eat or drink, but Kenna had limited her caffeine consumption as soon as she'd started accidentally lighting fires and discovered she had a bun in the oven.

Lizzie swallowed back a yawn as she made her way down the steps to the basement. If she wasn't pregnant, then she'd have Frank check for anything else that might cause exhaustion, food cravings, and excessive senti-mentality.

Anything besides not getting enough sleep and trying

to save her corner of the world. But that stuff wasn't really new to her.

Harrington paused at the bottom of the stairs and looked up at her. "You're certain you don't want—"

"If you ask me about seeing Frank one more time, I *will* suffocate you." He'd already mentioned it four times. Four refusals later, and she was ready to commit a little violence. "Or maybe I'll just shove you into a nearby wall. I hear neither is pleasant, and I'm handy at both."

Pilar planned to meet Harrington and Lizzie outside the room where the book was stored. Lizzie only hoped her friend and mentor wouldn't go quite so cuckoo as Harrington. Better yet, that she'd never know, because maybe Harrington would keep his mouth shut.

"Frank?" Pilar called out from the basement. "Lizzie, why do you need to see Frank?"

Just Lizzie's luck that Pilar had beat them downstairs. As soon as she turned the corner, she saw Pilar's concerned face. "I'm fine, which is why I don't need to see Frank. Harrington is being an old man."

Pilar pinched her lips together. "Not that it's polite to ask, but aren't you in your forties, Harrington?"

"It's a figure of speech," Lizzie said. Her exasperation made her tone of sharper than she'd intended. "Will you two give me a break? My...situation is none of your business, Harrington. And you"—she pointed a finger at Pilar—"don't encourage him."

Pilar gave her a curious look, then her mouth opened slightly. "You're finally pregnant, aren't you?"

"Finally?" Lizzie glared—at Pilar, at Harrington, at the closed door behind which the evil book lurked. "I'd ask what the hell that means, but we have other concerns at the moment. Do either one of you lunatics have a plan?"

Harrington and Pilar shared a commiserating look.

"No plan?" Lizzie asked. "All righty, then. I'll have a stab."

And before either of the raging idiots next to her could complain, she opened the door to reveal the necromancy book.

Dead bugs buzzed around her face, crawled on the floor, and in general annoyed her about as much as her well-meaning boss and mentor.

She turned her ire toward the black book on the pedestal. Next, she started to think in exactly the way that made Harrington and Pilar twitch: out of the box.

She cast a wider net this time with her ward, one that encompassed the entire room. And she didn't work through the steps of magic—one, two, and three—fluidly. No, she let her freak flag fly, and she ripped the magic from her body and flung it across the room.

It spread in a wide swath, lighting up the room with shiny sparkles—and also capturing all of the flying bugs in its net.

Literally capturing them. They hung suspended in midair, shining with varying degrees of brightness.

Unlike the sensing ward Lizzie had cast on the Lycan, the bugs didn't show any outward signs of distress. They formed a shiny grid of magic secondary to the ward Lizzie cast.

"What in the holy hell is that?" Harrington asked.

Lizzie examined the varying shades and brightness of

the grid formed by the glowing bug bodies. They looked like an incomprehensible mishmash of lights, but then she blinked. In that brief moment when her eyes first opened and before she'd fully focused, she saw the pattern.

"Oh. My. God." Lizzie traced a pattern in the air with her finger. "It's a path."

"More like a stream," Harrington replied as he dodged and weaved through the frozen bugs, following the brightest of them.

"Lizzie," Pilar said tentatively. "How did you freeze the bugs?"

"I'm haven't a clue." Lizzie thought back to her formation of intent, but it was fuzzy. She'd rushed through the familiar steps so quickly, and she'd been so peeved—angry, really—that she hadn't clearly formed her intent. Except that wasn't how magic worked. If any of the three pieces failed—the magical power, the clearly expressed intent, or the will to implement—then no ward was cast, no distance faded, no magic happened.

Which meant she'd formulated a plan of attack for her ward somewhere in the depths of her mind. She poked and prodded but found only a tangle of unpleasant emotions: frustration with Harrington for his persistent and unwanted concern, annoyance that her mentor and friend had expected her to get the baby bug well before she'd given it much thought herself, and a terrible loneliness that only John could fill.

John—his absence was the real problem. She wanted her damn mate. She wanted to know if she was pregnant, but not without him by her side, holding her hand.

She wanted Elin and her petty, vicious, self-centered play for power squashed like one of the frozen, glowing bugs she couldn't take her eyes off.

She tapped one of the bugs with the tip of her finger, and it fell to the ground.

"Lizzie!" Pilar cried.

Harrington's groan of frustration made Lizzie feel perversely satisfied. "Can you not play with the bugs until we sort out how stable this ward is?"

Hands on her hips, Lizzie remarked on what was now obvious: "I don't see a change. What about y'all?"

Neither of her partners in crime replied. Their silence spoke volumes, though, and she decided sorting out the kind of magic she'd conjured up before she tinkered with it wasn't a *terrible* idea.

If her memory failed to yield results, then perhaps her eyes would do a better job. Or simply the feel of the thing. Working magic was part skill (gained through training and experience) and part intuition.

She put a pin in the question of her pregnancy, opened her eyes, and let herself feel the magic.

A handful of heartbeats passed, and then she felt it. The cool whisper of wind on her cheek. No... The cool slide of water around her body.

"Whoa. I can feel it." Harrington retained an air of equanimity most of the time, so seeing him surprised was a treat. "Like a pleasantly warm spring."

"It figures the British guy thinks it's warm." Lizzie closed her eyes and let herself float with the gentle current. Not literally—her feet were moving—but it felt like floating.

"I'm following you lunatics, because we can only go so far in an enclosed room," Pilar said as she trailed behind. "But Lizzie's right. It's the temperature of the Caribbean on a warm fall day. Not cold, just cool enough to be refreshing."

Lizzie stopped in the corner of the room, her retinue close behind. She tapped the wall. "The main library is on the other side, right?"

"Yes," Pilar and Harrington said simultaneously.

Lizzie grasped their hands and, without asking permission—she really was channeling Kenna these days—she faded to the other side.

Pilar's eyes rounded when she saw where they'd landed, namely the other side of a very solid wall.

Harrington was more vocal. He spat out a few curses, then said, "You do need me alive. If I'm dead, I can't help Kenna or Gwen."

"Please. You look fine to me." Fading disoriented the uninitiated, and it was incredibly bad manners to cart someone around magically without permission, but they were on the clock. Lizzie dropped their hands before addressing the more pressing question. "Any thoughts on how we turn off the tap? Or do we need to find the source to do that?"

She hoped not, because the wellspring could be buried in solid rock or dirt or—

"Oh, I don't think you'll have much luck deciphering either of those riddles."

Elin.

10

———

"PPC is under attack, and they send for *you*." Elin's scathing comment and all of her attention were directed at Lizzie. "You're nothing."

Lizzie found the fresh-faced, rosy-cheeked, blonde Elin downright disturbing.

Maybe it was the discordant contrast between the light tones of the teenage girl whose body had been usurped and the vile words escaping her mouth?

As Lizzie scrambled for something to say—now would be a great time to pick the evil bad guy's brain—she was sidetracked by a flash of movement in her peripheral vision.

Harrington's body made a dull thud as he slammed into the wall next to her. He fell forward in a heap before she could catch him.

Who was she kidding? Catch him? She hadn't seen it coming or even understood what had happened, not until Elin said, "Uh, uh, uh. No calling the dragons for reinforcements, Mr. Bossman."

Elin lifted her hand and slowly closed her fist.

A choking noise emerged from Harrington's doubled-over figure. Elin was squeezing the life from him.

Shit. Lizzie better jump-start her brain cells fast.

She said the first thing that popped in her head. "What brought you out of hiding? The dragons had you on the run, so something must have changed."

Elin giggled. It seemed the idea that she was hiding from anyone, dragon clan or otherwise, was funny to her. Fine with Lizzie, since Elin had stopped squeezing the life from Harrington.

Distract, maybe that was the key. Get her talking, and she wouldn't be so eager to thwack the three of them against any available hard surface or choke them...or kill them in any fashion and have them join the undead army she was building.

That lit a fire under Lizzie's ass, and she started talking, letting anything that popped into her head pass through her lips.

"How'd you get on the possession life track, Elin? Can I call you Elin? Or do you prefer your nymph name?"

"Elin is just fine. And I like not dying—how about you?"

Flawed plan, very flawed plan, Lizzie realized as Elin pointed a finger at her heart. A piercing pain stole her breath and tears welled in her eyes.

There was a time not so long ago when a viable plan would have popped into Lizzie's head. Hadn't she read somewhere that pregnant women could be forgetful? She pounded the wall with her fist. Not only was she likely knocked up, but her brain cells were on a temporary hiatus until her (theoretical) baby was fully cooked.

The pain faded, but only because she was getting lightheaded. *Oh, Lord.* She really needed to get her shit together. To reel in the crazy and get herself sorted. John would never forgive her if she got killed. And she'd never forgive herself. For all she knew, her spirit would get stuck in the library like Matylda's, and then she'd have decades, centuries, to feel guilty.

Amidst the baby bomb, the ancient madwoman threat, John, Harrington, Pilar, and several tangents related to each, her focus managed to flit through an improbable number of topics. Finally, it skittered by one helpful thought: shield.

Whether it would work against whatever magic Elin was using, Lizzie didn't know. She didn't give a flying fuck. It was her only option.

Lizzie yanked her magic and flung. Like before, when she'd chucked her magic in a fit of pique, there were no steps. It was all instinct, and she really hoped somewhere in that process she'd hit on all the required parts.

She did. Oh, boy, did she.

The shield she'd hastily cast tingled and sparked as it settled across all three of them. Her brain was pretty awesome on autopilot; it even remembered to protect her friends.

A familiar scent wafted in the air, distracting her from her newfound speed-casting talent. If her imagination hadn't been running mad and her brain wasn't on the fritz, she'd have sworn she smelled John.

"You bitch," Elin snarled.

She flung a ball of fire—a freaking ball of fire—at Lizzie, but the shield held. In fact, it flared even brighter.

Lizzie could feel Harrington's magic poking at the shield. "You've tapped into the wellspring."

"Um, no," Lizzie said. "I don't know how to do that."

"Lizzie," Pilar said, "you did. And you better figure out how you did, because my shield didn't hold against Elin's hybrid magic."

Of course Pilar and Harrington had been protecting themselves and each other. Lizzie had been the only one having a meltdown. If this was pregnancy brain, she didn't want it. Wow, that moved from theoretical to probable awfully fast in her head.

"Lizzie!" Pillar poked her in the side. "Pay attention. She's over there muttering some incantation I'm not familiar with."

"She's attempting to deconstruct the shield." Harrington rolled his right shoulder and winced. "That or she's attempting to deconstruct us. It's hard to tell. I'm only catching every few words."

"What do you expect me to do?" Lizzie stared at the ward she'd only seconds earlier cobbled together. It didn't feel different from the wards she'd cast in the past. All magic had a feel to it, and this felt like hers.

Harrington took a deep breath, winced, schooled his features into a mask of calm, then began to speak to her like she was a baby spell caster. Even worse, she appreciated it. "Both your sensing ward and your shield tapped into the wellspring. Consider what you did when you cast those wards."

She nodded. Easy. She'd mindlessly thrown a bunch of magic in a fit of peevish anger.

He looked at her expectantly. His nostrils flared, and he said, "Perhaps you could share with us what that difference was."

"Quickly," Pilar added with a nervous glance at the still-muttering Elin.

"Right. I was frustrated, impatient, and not thinking very clearly. For whatever reason." Lizzie skipped over the whys and went straight to the result. "I didn't carefully craft a goal or target for my magic. I let my intent run a bit wild and sort itself out."

Harrington blinked. "Sort itself out."

She nodded.

"You threw magic out into the ether...and hoped it would work out." Harrington looked heavenward.

At times like this, Lizzie wondered if he was praying, asking forgiveness for his sins, begging for patience, or if he just liked to stare at the ceiling when she (or Kenna) tried his patience.

"In my defense, I had sensing ward on the brain before, and there wasn't much floating around in my grey matter besides not dying when I cast the shield ward."

Pilar snorted. "I didn't teach her that."

"No," Harrington replied, then turned to Lizzie and said, "Do it."

"Do what?"

"Whatever you must to stop Elin. She's seconds from finishing her deconstruction incantation. Pilar's and my magic is useless against her." And in true Harrington fashion, he added a touch of intimidation at just the right moment. He wrapped his left hand around her arm and squeezed hard. "Now, if you'd like to live."

So she did.

11

———

Lizzie struggled with moral choices. Meaning she wanted to make them, but there seemed to be an awful lot of grey in what many saw as black and white.

Right, wrong, or the winding road between the two. She didn't always know where she landed, just did her best to make the right choice in that moment when the choice had to be made.

She preferred to walk the straight and narrow, but her mate broke human laws with few qualms. She chose to love him. Right, wrong? It was the right choice for her. She believed it when she made the choice, and even more so now.

Lizzie had wanted to help Kenna save her mother, yet here she was dealing with a nymph possession, bugpocalypse, and a zombie Lycan. She had no idea if Kenna was safe, if Gwen was still alive, or if they'd all come home safe—but here she was, miles and miles away. Lizzie hoped it was the right choice, but it was the best one she could make.

And then there was Elin. A young woman from Norway, innocent of the heinous acts the nymph had perpetrated. The nymph had dabbled in the taboo magics of re-animation and mind control, certainly, but had also quite possibly committed murder. Ewan's staff had yet to reach Elin's aunt Emme, and they feared the worst.

All of these thoughts existed in a hazy swirl in Lizzie's brain as she once more forcefully thrust her magic upon the world with no clear intent formed. Magic, hell yes. She had plenty. And will? She wanted to live, so that was abundant.

But to what end would her magic be used? Murky, poorly clarified intent yielded...what?

Something completely unexpected. Bizarre, since the idea must have come from somewhere in her head.

Elin collapsed in a graceless heap on the floor—but only after an ethereal, vaporous, vaguely humanlike figure separated from her.

If that didn't make Lizzie's mind spin, the image of a dragon—a very large, scaly dragon, one with monstrous claws and wicked fangs—appeared as a superimposed image over the familiar human form of Ewan.

In her head, a voice whispered, "Drop the shield, Lizzie."

Like her head wasn't jacked enough as it was. Whether it was exhaustion, stress, or baby brain, she hadn't been in tiptop form lately, but until now she hadn't been hearing voices. Voices telling her to make herself vulnerable to attack. Um...no.

"It's Ewan. We need you to drop the shield," the creepy voice in her head said while she watched the silvery, human-shaped fog drift further away from Elin. "Now!"

Bullshit that was Ewan. It had to be a ploy by the nymph. She'd probably possess one of them once the shield was dropped.

"It's not bullshit, and stop screaming. You're making my head hurt." The voice sounded grumpy...and a lot like Ewan.

Lizzie laughed hysterically, and then she dropped the shield.

The moment it flared, a flash of dragon fire surrounded the nymph's form and she...evaporated? Fell apart?

Lizzie couldn't quite figure it out, and it seemed like an awful lot of effort right now. Her head wanted to float away, and the edges of her vision were narrowing with alarming speed.

Shit. She was going to pass out.

12

———

Lizzie woke up in a familiar place, in her bed in her assigned room at the IPPC library in Prague. Which would normally be fine—good, even—and yet it felt all sorts of wrong and she couldn't remember why.

"Hey." The deep rumble of John's achingly familiar voice made her heart tumble.

He wasn't supposed to be here, she was pretty sure. She was also sure that hearing him and looking at his tired, unshaven, but still impossibly handsome face shouldn't make her cry.

But it did. Big, fat tears fell down her face, then they fell even faster when she couldn't figure out why she was crying.

He didn't say anything. He sat down on the edge of her bed, gathered her up in his arms, and held her.

Eventually, the tears slowed and then stopped. "I'm sorry. I don't even know why I'm crying."

He tucked her head under his chin and rubbed slow circles across her back, but he didn't say anything.

After a few minutes of silence, it dawned on her that she'd probably upset him. He *hated* to see her cry.

She nuzzled into his chest. "I'm fine. Promise."

"Um-hm. What's the last thing you remember?" he whispered in her ear, like he was afraid his raised voice would trigger more tears.

"I don't know." Which was odd. She didn't remember going to bed. Didn't remember walking up the stairs, what she ate for dinner...why John was here. "Wait, you're supposed to be in Texas."

That much she knew. He was in Texas, and she'd taken an IPPC case in Prague. She'd taken the case outside of her normal schedule when John couldn't travel with her, because... She grabbed at the elusive memories. "Right! Because of Gwen. Oh, Gwen. Did Kenna—"

"She's fine. Kenna, Gwen, Max, and their team—everyone's home and fine."

Lizzie's memories came back in a flood. "The nymph, Elin..."

"Elin's fine and the nymph is gone." When Lizzie leaned back so she could look at his face, he added, "For good."

Something was off. About him and the way he was acting. He was too subdued. Restrained, quiet. And when one last precious memory clicked into place, his odd demeanor assumed a newly ominous meaning.

"Our baby." Her hand flew to her stomach, and she looked down—as if there would be some evidence there of the horrible truth. "Oh my God. I lost the baby, didn't I?"

Huge, racking sobs tore through her body, and she reached blindly for comfort. She clung to John as a horrible, tangled mix of guilt and sorrow consumed her.

"Lizzie!" John shook her. From the look on his face, she'd guess it wasn't the first time he'd call her name. "You didn't lose the baby."

"What? What!" She smacked his arm. "And you let me sit here and bawl like a..." Like a bereaved mother with megawattage guilt, but she couldn't say that out loud.

John was eyeing her intently. "You want to be pregnant?"

He looked heartbreakingly hopeful.

"I don't know, sneaky scent sniffer. What do you think?" She might be playing cool and calm, but she was a bundle of nerves.

This wasn't at all how she'd envisioned John finding out she was pregnant.

Hell, she hadn't even been sure she was knocked up until she'd seen the look on his face. She'd wanted them to take the test together. To find out together, as a couple.

"Um, if I'm A-okay, then what's with the fuzzy memory and the passing out?"

A grim look replaced his happy daddy face. "Remember when you faded further than any sane person would attempt?"

Oh, yeah. She remembered that. Using too much magic at once was a really bad idea. It wiped a gal out, laid her up in bed for ages, and... "Oh. Oops. I used too much magic?" She peeked up and flashed him a sheepish grin.

"Yes."

She nodded.

Fair enough. She deserved a few grumpy looks. Though she hadn't done it on purpose, that wouldn't matter to her if the roles were reversed and John showed up in an equally sad state. She'd still be peeved.

"Wanna tell me why you were so stressed when I woke up?"

He bumped her over in the bed. When there was room for him to stretch out, he pulled her into his lap and hugged her close. He nuzzled her neck and kissed her lightly. "I wasn't sure how you felt about..." He shoved his nose against her neck and inhaled, then sighed.

"You were afraid I wouldn't be happy about having your baby?" She leaned back to look at his face. Unlike some, she didn't have the ability to smell emotions. What she saw floored her. He looked uncertain, worried.

"We haven't exactly discussed a timeline."

"No, that's true." She pulled his head down and kissed him.

When their lips met, she told him the best way she knew how that he was everything. That their baby was a cherished gift. That she couldn't be happier, planned or not. That she loved him with all her heart.

Sometimes with Lycan, words didn't quite cut it.

She suspected they'd have done a little more than kiss if she hadn't been laid out by magic overuse and they both didn't have some serious follow-up meetings to attend to downstairs. But she thought it was enough.

When he grinned down at her, she was sure of it.

"I'm glad you're happy."

"Not happy, thrilled. Ecstatic. Over the moon." She leaned against him and snuggled close. A deep sense of contentment filled her—right up until her tired brain did a logistics leap without her consent. That was when her heart started to race, her palms sweated, and her mouth went suddenly dry. "Oh my God. My parents."

"It's fine. We'll bump up the wedding."

She snorted. "You think I'm worried about the wedding?" She laughed with the hysteria of the truly panicked. "John, I'm going to have to tell them you're Lycan."

His sharp bark of laughter held a good deal more amusement than hers had.

13

———

Not five minutes passed after Lizzie's horrid discovery—that priority for "the talk" with her parents had been shifted to code red—when Ewan knocked on her door.

"The boss would like to debrief you before you leave." After John gave him the nod, Ewan grinned and extended his hand. "Congratulations on your news."

Her hand hovered briefly over her stomach as she shook his hand. "Thank you." Turning to John, she asked, "Are we leaving soon?

"Plane's on standby," he replied. "Frank wants to check you over one more time before we leave, answer any questions you might have—"

"*We* might have."

John's lips twitched, but he just nodded and wrapped an arm around her.

"All right, then. Let's get this over with. I want to go

home." She hadn't meant to sound quite so pathetic with that last bit, but it was what it was: she was homesick.

When they entered the library, it was to find Harrington decked out in a sling.

"Don't tell me you pissed off Frank," she said. She could have bit her tongue. Not only was the statement rude in the general sense, but as soon as she said it, she realized why Harrington hadn't been healed. Frank had expended all of his magical reserve speeding along *her* recovery. "I'm sorry. I've been in a mood for days now."

Harrington chose this moment to act the complete gentleman. Naturally, when it would make her feel like a complete heel. He offered his left hand and hearty congratulations.

Once Ewan and Harrington had toasted her pregnancy with obscenely expensive thirty-year-old Laphroaig (John refrained, since she couldn't join in), they got down to business.

Ewan gave her the quick and dirty details. He and Tavish had come running the moment they'd heard her panicked cries for help via telepathy.

"I know," Lizzie said. "I think too loud."

Ewan shrugged. "A saving grace in this instance. When we arrived, we found you'd managed to separate the nymph from her host."

"And Elin, she's..."

"Quite well," Harrington replied. "Thankfully, she has no memory after she was possessed up to the point the nymph released her body. She's already home with her family."

"How did you know to separate them?" Ewan asked.

She shook her head, confused by the question, so he clarified. "That's the only weakness Matylda could discover: a vulnerability to water and fire in their natural state."

"Oh! Matylda! How is she? Where is she?" Illogical as it was, Lizzie had the urge to scan the room for signs of her corporeal or ghostly forms.

"Gone. She left a note for you." Harrington retrieved it and slid it across his desk. "I found it on my desk."

It was strange to see her own name scrawled across the envelope in Matylda's handwriting. She tucked it in her pocket for later.

"How did you know, Lizzie, to separate the nymph from her host?" Ewan asked again.

"I didn't. I just didn't want to hurt Elin. I also think my magic has been on the fritz since a certain Lycan knocked me up."

John's lips twitched again. If she knew her guy, he was getting a kick out of being reminded he'd impregnated his mate. Yeah, he was a Neanderthal, but only in the most innocuous ways. Also, the guy had super sperm. They'd had unprotected sex once. *One time.* She shook her head.

"I have a theory about that," Harrington said.

Lizzie blushed, but then she realized he hadn't read her mind. He was talking about her magic and not John's super sperm.

"Do tell," John said in a way that made it clear he had a good idea what she'd been thinking. He clasped her hand and twined their fingers. "Tell us all about Lizzie's magic."

She shot him a warning look, which he returned with an oh-so-innocent "who, me?" look.

"I think it has something to do with carrying a Lycan child. I think your magic might be altered while you're pregnant."

"But not after?" Because she might just decide to go on a little sabbatical from magic, if that was the case.

"I'm not sure, but that's my guess," Harrington said. "Frank agrees, but again, we're not certain."

Lizzie knew that Lycan didn't interbreed with non-Lycan often, but they did. And when they did, it was usually with spell casters. Specifically, record keepers, her particular type of spell caster. So there shouldn't be any big mysteries...but with magic, who knew?

"When are you guys going to get to the good stuff?" Lizzie asked. She was a homesick pregnant gal, and she hadn't had the opportunity to properly greet her soon-to-be-husband yet. This show needed to get rolling. She crossed her arms. "Zombies? A wellspring that's sprung a leak?"

"Ah." Ewan nodded. "The zombies self-resolved. No nymph, no zombies."

"Right, so it's all magically okay?" She groaned internally. She was getting punny. Or was that just bad humor?

"No," Harrington said. "It's all been managed with good planning and an excellent eye for detail. That is how *some* of IPPC's employees operate."

Lizzie rolled her eyes. Okay, not really, but she thought about doing it. Someone's delicate sensibilities were offended by her hastily constructed wards. It wasn't her usual MO, but it had worked.

Ewan filled in the blanks when Harrington didn't: "We've moved the book to another—highly classified—location, away from the wellspring."

"As for the wellspring, we've engaged the help of the witching community to contain and study it." Harrington couldn't hide his excitement over the prospect. He was an IPPC recruitment machine. Larger geographic areas, greater numbers, new magic-using communities added to the fold—all goals that Harrington worked tirelessly to achieve. He'd love to get the witching community more involved with IPPC. The not crazy ones, anyway.

"Gwen?" Lizzie asked. Because it sure as hell wouldn't be any witch with a Coven of Light affiliation.

"Yes," Harrington said. "And her people." He paused, considering Lizzie and John. His gaze skimmed quickly over their clasped hands. "If you don't have any other questions, I'll consider this debrief concluded."

He and Ewan wished John and her safe travels.

Once they were in the hallway, John tugged her hand until she stopped. "Read it now."

The letter had been burning a hole in her pocket since she stashed it. She shot him a grateful look, then retrieved it. It wasn't long, just a few lines.

Dear Lizzie,

I believe my spirit may not remain on this plane once my body returns to dust. In case I do not have the opportunity to tell you before I leave, I want you to know: I am proud to call you niece. To discover my family line continued was a surprise. To discover you was a joy.

With love,
Your Aunt Matylda

LIZZIE TUCKED the letter back in her pocket, then twisted the sapphire ring on her finger. "She knew. She knew she wasn't coming back as a ghost." Lizzie shrugged. "Or she suspected, anyway. She just wanted to say goodbye."

"That was decent of her."

Lizzie nodded. "Yeah. It really was." She shook her head. "Let's go home."

John tucked her against his side. "Yeah, let's go home."

"Mom, Dad. It's so great to see you." Lizzie hugged her parents.

"Well, sweetheart, you did make it sound quite urgent." Her mom glanced at Lizzie's midsection.

A glance she would firmly ignore. She smiled pleasantly at her mother.

Why was it taking John so long to retrieve her parents' luggage from their car?

She forced herself to neither look at nor touch her stomach. Her hands would remain firmly at her sides, and she would not give away the fact that she and John had let one slip past the goalie.

This visit was about *one* big reveal.

Magic was enough of a bomb to drop. The pregnancy could wait another month until she was further along. Also, if things went poorly today and her parents freaked out, she could use the pregnancy as an enticement for reconciliation. Her mother was mad for a grandchild.

Working so much with Harrington had certainly left its mark. Now she was plotting out contingency plans for her personal relationships.

John appeared in the hallway, looking like he was struggling a bit with their three large bags. "Ronald, Evelyn, I'll go ahead and take your bags to your room."

Please. The man could carry twice that all day and not break a sweat. Even if he wasn't Lycan, he was a big guy.

He caught her eye and dropped a slow, sly wink. The jerk. She had to swallow back a laugh.

"Let's grab a cup of tea." Herding her parents into the kitchen and then preparing their drinks kept her nerves in check. John returned just as she was setting out cups.

She'd been mentally ticking off all the "issues" her parents would soon be struggling with: living in sin with a man she hadn't known very long (according to her parents' math), knocked up and unwed, and co-habiting with a guy who wasn't entirely human. So it was a good thing he appeared when he did.

No telling which way this could roll. If only her parents weren't quite so clueless about their own heritage, this would be so much easier.

"Are you going to tell us whatever it is you want to tell us, or are we going to pretend like nothing unusual is going on here?" Her dad, lord love him, never one to beat about the bush.

"Ronald!" Her mother smacked his chest. "We talked about this. You have to let them tell us in their own time."

Now that was a shocking statement coming from her nosy mother.

But then her mom ruined the moment and said, "But if now is the time, that would be lovely." She folded her hands in her lap and gave Lizzie an expectant look.

John, the unhelpful ass, was cracking up. Not that her parents would notice. The lip-twitching and eye-crinkling were as far as it got, but he'd be laughing out loud if he didn't think it would offend her parents.

She shot him a baleful look. "John has something he wants to tell you."

That put a crimp in his amusement.

He leaned back in his chair and crossed his arms. "I do?"

Nodding, Lizzie said, "Yep. Go right ahead." Turning to her parents, she said, "I love you."

If she was letting John handle this—and he should; he owed her given the division of labor for childbirth—then she needed to get a proactive declaration of her devotion in with her parents before the everything went pear shaped.

John arched an eyebrow. She could read between the lines: you asked for it.

Then he said, "I love your daughter. More than anyone else on this earth. She means the world to me, and I hope you understand that what I am doesn't change that."

Wow, good opener. Much more discreet than she'd expected.

Except her dad was turning funny colors. "Son, if you're going to start talking politics and religion, I'll stop you now. We don't abide with any of these off the grid, end of days groups. You're not taking our little girl to live in a bunker under the ground away from all her people."

He was even turning a funny shade of purple Lizzie hadn't seen since prom night. He'd been really angry prom night. It took a second for the meaning of his words to sink in, and she was choking back a startled laugh by the time John replied.

"No, sir." John didn't address whatever it was that her dad thought he might be. He just dropped the truth bomb. "I'm Lycan—a werewolf."

Silence descended.

Then her dad let out a sigh of relief. "Well thank the heavens for that. I thought you were going to tell me that place of yours out in Smithville was some kind of compound and you two were going underground."

Just as Lizzie snapped her mouth shut—because what the hell?—her mom smacked her dad on the chest again and said, "You didn't tell me about werewolves."

Her brain was going to explode. "What. The. Hell."

Her dad rubbed the back of his neck and winced. "I guess maybe we should have had the Talk."

She squinted at him, trying to decide if she should murder him now or is patricide was a step too far. John saved the day. She'd thank him someday. Not today, but someday.

"Sir, are you saying you're aware of the existence of magic?"

"Hm, yes," Ronald Smith, the man who'd raised her and never breathed a word of her magical heritage, nodded like it was no big deal. "Hard not to have some inkling given my heritage. The Kovars are a big deal. Well, they used to be, back before we anglicized our name."

Lizzie snorted. "So I hear."

Her dad frowned. "Your mother and I decided not to share that part of my family history when it became clear that, like me, you hadn't inherited the family's special talents."

John squeezed her hand. "But she did."

Oops. He didn't say it, but it was written across his face. "We were trying to save you unnecessary fear as a child. Magic can be a terrifying influence as a child."

Hand-squeezing wasn't doing the job, so John pulled Lizzie into his lap and cuddled her. If her parents didn't like, well, tough. They could just deal.

"So, a werewolf?" her mom asked. "You seem—" She. Swallowed whatever she'd been about to say.

To give her credit, she was doing better than Lizzie had when she'd learned the truth about John. She remembered making some kind of comment about excessive hair or pointy ears. Maybe teeth. There had definitely been a big, bad wolf theme to the conversation.

"Lycan, Mom, that's what they're called. They're not really werewolves."

"I see." And she nodded her head like she did, when it was clear she hadn't a clue. Again, kudos to her, because she didn't seem too terribly upset by what some parents might deem Bad News. But then her face scrunched up with displeasure, and she gave me one of her disappointed looks. "Does this mean you're *not* pregnant?"

Lizzie leaned back against John's chest, closed her eyes, and laughed. Relief, frustration, joy—it all swished around inside of her.

John wrapped his arms around her and said, "Ronald, Evelyn, we hope you'll be amongst the first to congratulate us. We're pregnant."

Lizzie cuddled her guy, kissed him like her parents weren't in the room (and didn't even feel bad about it), and then she accepted her parents' heartfelt congratulations.

The End

For more adventures in the Lost Library world, check out
Spirelli Paranormal Investigations.
Keep reading for an excerpt!

ALSO BY KATE BARAY

LOST LIBRARY

Lost Library

Spirited Legacy

Defensive Magic

Witch's Diary

Necromancy

LOST LIBRARY SHORTS

Krampus Gone Wild: A Lost Library Christmas Short

The Covered Mirror: A Lost Library Halloween Short

LOST LIBRARY COLLECTIONS

Lost Library Collection: Books 1-3

Lost Library Short Story Collection

SPIRELLI PARANORMAL INVESTIGATIONS

The Disappearing Client

The Forgotten Memories

The Fleeing Witch

Something Nasty in the Attic

The Geolocating Book

The Heartbeat in the House

SPIRELLI PARANORMAL INVESTIGATIONS COLLECTIONS

Spirelli Paranormal Investigations: Episodes 1-3

Spirelli Paranormal Investigations: Episodes 4-6

SPIRELLI

Entombed

BOB VS THE WORLD

Bob vs the Cat

ABOUT THE AUTHOR

When Kate's not tapping away at her keyboard or in deep contemplation of her next fanciful writing project, she's sweeping up hairy dust bunnies and watching British mysteries.

She lives with her pack of pointers and hounds, some of whom make appearances in her books, in Boise, Idaho.

She's worked as an attorney, a dog trainer, and in various other positions, but writer is the hands-down winner.

She hopes you enjoy reading her stories as much as she loves writing them!

THE DISAPPEARING CLIENT EXCERPT

Jack fiddled with the inner workings of his ancient cash register. He needed a newer machine to better track sales, because—surprisingly—The Junk Shop actually had a few sales to track.

Who knew boxes of garage sale rejects would be so popular? The store hours were erratic, and the stock ranged from recycled trash to bizarre trinkets, yet the store still received stellar online consumer reviews. It didn't have a website. So how did the yuppies, hipsters— whoever the hell was writing the reviews—find it?

"You know, that car outside looks like it needs a little work. I might know a guy, if you're interested."

Five foot and a lot, the woman attached to the voice would be hard to miss, with her fiery red hair and overly bright green eyes.

Jack left his barstool perch behind the counter and had a long look at her. He'd missed her entering the store, and her voice had startled him. Quite a task, considering he had a tight ward on the store, and he was hardly an unobservant guy.

"How can I help you?" Jack worked to produce a convincingly relaxed tone.

Face expressionless, the redhead said, "I'm here to apply for the position."

"We're not hiring at the moment." When she didn't reply and she also didn't leave, he added, "Look around. We're a small shop, but maybe something will catch your eye."

Sure, The Junk Shop was a retail location, but it had begun primarily as a front for Jack's work with the magic-using community. A discreet physical location was a bonus when meeting with clients who wanted to stay under the radar. He looked around the small store. For a front, it was becoming increasingly and uncomfortably popular.

She looked around. "Uh-huh. I'm not here for . . . bric-a-brac. I'm sure you've got a position open. My sources are excellent."

Jack hadn't posted the position. Where would he? He could just imagine how that ad would read. *Wanted: Paranormal investigator's assistant. Complete discretion and some ass-kicking required. Part-time help in The Junk Shop mandatory. A high tolerance for the unexplainable preferred.* No.

And Jack had only mentioned to a select few that he was looking to hire: his highest-ranking Inter-Pack Policing Cooperative contact, Harrington; the Texas Pack leader, John Braxton; and IPPC's temporary chief of security for the Prague library, Ewan Campbell.

"Who's your reference?"

"My stealth entry into the store wasn't reference enough?" She gave him a toothy smile.

That smile made him incredibly uncomfortable. Green eyes, creepy feeling—alarm bells were ringing. Fuck. His stealthy, green-eyed Amazon was a dragon. He'd bet cash on it. He stared back without answering.

She shrugged. "Lachlan McClellan, but that might not be entirely to my benefit when you check my references."

"Head of the McClellan clan?"

The guy led a powerful clan of dragons, but he was also a dick with a crap sense of humor. And Jack didn't see him being particularly enlightened about female employees. Although he was surprised Ewan had mentioned Jack's staffing needs to his clan leader.

She hesitated before responding. "We're from the same clan."

Oh, fuck—dragon. He knew it. "You want the job?"

She raised an eyebrow. "I'm here, having this conversation with you."

Her non-answers were annoying as hell. More importantly, he didn't see them becoming less annoying with time and proximity.

"Pass." Jack turned back to the register.

"Wait. Yes, I would like the job." She continued to speak to his back. "Please. I would very much like this job."

Slowly Jack turned around. "Then tell me why I should hire you? Besides your stealth entry into a warded store. That only tells me you're a thief."

A brief flicker of fiery green flashed in her eyes, but

quickly dimmed. "I'm unemployed and unable to return to my previous employer, which makes me highly motivated to be successful here. Also, I understand you're looking for muscle. My combat skills are excellent." She blinked. "I can demonstrate."

She gave him another smile with just a shade too many teeth.

"No thanks. A dragon kicking my very human ass isn't much of a demonstration. Besides, I'd hate for us to break my bric-a-brac." Jack sat down behind the counter and picked up a pen. Having a dragon would be a huge tactical advantage in most fights, regardless of technical competence.

"Talk to Lachlan. Whatever else he might say, he'll tell you I'm honest and hardworking." She placed a slight emphasis on "honest." She swallowed, the first sign of nervousness she'd displayed since walking into his store. "Please."

Apparently he'd hit a nerve when he'd compared her to a thief. A highly motivated, well-connected dragon employee—he'd be an idiot to walk away just because she wasn't exactly right. Especially since he didn't know what "exactly right" was. What type of person wouldn't drive him nuts with continuous contact? The shelf life of most of his relationships, regardless of the type, was pretty short.

"What's your name?"

"Marin." She didn't offer her hand.

Jack knew the right answer, yet still he hesitated. Damn. He had a job coming up day after tomorrow that could use some dragon muscle.

"All right, Marin. Come back tomorrow at ten. If your reference comes through, we'll discuss employment terms." He narrowed his eyes. "I don't pay well."

She ducked her chin once in acknowledgment and headed out the door. This time, Jack saw her pass through the ward, and a shower of green sparks, visible only to him, fell in her wake. He felt a corresponding pinch from the ring he wore on his right hand. No way he'd missed the ward triggering when she'd first entered the store. If this whole thing worked out and she joined Spirelli Paranormal Investigations, that was one of his first questions.

Jack picked up his cell and scrolled through his contacts, looking for Ewan's number. Jack was pretty sure Ewan would put him in touch with Lachlan. After a quick mental calculation, adding seven hours to account for Prague time, Jack decided it wasn't too late and dialed Ewan's number.

Ewan answered on the first ring. "Jack. What's up?"

"Hey, Ewan. Any chance you could put me in touch with Lachlan? I had someone come by the shop asking about that assistant's job. Remember, I told you I was looking for someone? Lachlan came up as a reference."

"Sure." Background noise filtered in. "Heads up— you're on speaker."

"Thanks, man. You might actually know her; she's from your clan. A tall redhead named Marin?"

The background noise abruptly disappeared. Ewan must have turned the speaker function off and picked up his phone. "Yeah." The word came out so short, it almost sounded like a grunt.

Something about Marin had drastically changed the tone of their conversation. Jack contemplated for a split second whether to ask. He closed his eyes. Had he lost his mind?

After a few seconds of silence, Ewan said, "Marin is my daughter."

Jack sat on his favorite barstool, the one positioned in front of the shop's register. Careful to make his tone as neutral as possible, he said, "I didn't know that."

"Clearly."

Jack didn't get it. Ewan seemed pissed, but the guy hadn't said a word about not hiring his kid. Since Jack wasn't eager to get singed or mutilated due to an unfortunate miscommunication, clarification was the wisest course. "So, are you telling me you don't want me to hire her?"

"Not at all."

Jesus. Really? Jack rolled his shoulders. "Are you telling me you want me to hire her?"

"What did you want to know?" Ewan's voice had lost some of its edge.

"Uh, okay." Jack figured Ewan had enough patience for about two questions, so he erred on the side of caution and limited himself to one. "Would you recommend Marin for the job?"

"Yes. We done?"

Good enough.

"Yeah. Thanks again." As he pocketed his phone, he caught a flash of movement out of the corner of his eye.

Staring at the now empty shop floor, he said, "I know you're there, little guy. You better be glad I know what rat poison does." He couldn't commit to chemical warfare—even in the pursuit of pest control. It was a weird quirk. Whatever. People who used rat poison must not know what that shit did to the insides of an animal. He snorted. Or they just didn't like living with rats. "Fuzzball, you're damn lucky I don't actually live in this pit."

Jack shook his head. He really needed to stop talking to the rats. It probably made them feel welcome. But he couldn't resist one last warning. "You better not touch the coffee, Fuzzface."

Grab your copy of Spirelli Paranormal Investigations: Episodes 1-3 now!

www.ingramcontent.com/pod-product-compliance
Lightning Source LLC
Chambersburg PA
CBHW052104150726

48002CB00006B/2216